TALES FROM
THE FOLLY

TALES FROM THE FOLLY

A RIVERS OF LONDON
SHORT STORY COLLECTION

BEN AARONOVITCH

JABberwocky Literary Agency, Inc.

Tales from the Folly:
A Rivers of London Short Story Collection
Copyright © 2020 by Ben Aaronovitch
All rights reserved
Published in 2020 by JABberwocky Literary Agency, Inc.,
in association with Zeno Agency LTD.

Cover artwork and design by Jayel Draco.
Hand lettering by Patrick Knowles.

ISBN 978-1-625675-09-5

www.awfulagent.com/ebooks

Contents

Charlaine Harris on Rivers of London

Since I wait anxiously for Ben Aaronovitch's books to be released, I was tickled pink to be invited to write an introduction for this collection of his short stories.

Aaronovitch's Peter Grant is one of the warmest and most interesting characters in Urban Fantasy. Peter was born an outsider, so being even more of an outsider by dint of his discovered magical ability does not throw Peter off course. He's doing the job he was born to do, with the legendary Nightingale as his mentor.

We can only stand by and watch breathlessly as Peter copes with bizarre situations, odd people, and creatures that have never been people.

Since we've become part of Peter's life and adventures, we get to meet the most interesting characters as soon as he does.

Ben Aaronovitch

I understand that the idea for Ben to write some short fiction in the Rivers of London world was originally Waterstones', so we have them to thank for coaxing Ben Aaronovitch to write much of this collection. I take my hat off to all those who encouraged him to let us have small adventures on top of big ones.

I know you'll enjoy these stories as much as I did.

—Charlaine Harris

Introduction to the Introductions

Welcome to the long-awaited Rivers of London short story collection. Like most people I almost never read the introductions to books, so will try and keep this as short, sweet and as useful as possible.

In this volume you will find all the short stories that I've written so far that are set in the world of Rivers of London. Most of them were published in special limited hardback editions for Waterstones and the Australian/ New Zealand market.

I started writing *Rivers of London* in 2008 in a desperate attempt to stave off bankruptcy. I really only have one talent and that's writing but my script writing career had gone bung and you cannot live unassisted in London on what you earn working as a bookseller. When the idea of Peter Grant, policeman, apprentice wizard and story magnet, coalesced in my mind I knew it was a goer—experience taught me that much—what I didn't know was that it was going to go so far. Several book deals later and I no longer have to hustle printed matter to survive—although I still find myself absentmindedly tidying up other people's bookshelves.

The short stories came about because of the 2012 Olympics for reasons I will detail below.

I have provided each short story with a brief introduction of its own and an indication of where it falls in the chronological sequence. And to answer your next question—what is the correct chronological order of the books? I have listed the order below…

Action at a Distance (Graphic novel #7)
Rivers of London (Strangely retitled *Midnight Riot* in the US)
Moon Over Soho
Whispers Under Ground
Broken Homes
Body Work (Graphic novel #1)
Foxglove Summer
What Abigail Did that Summer (Novella)
Night Witch (Graphic novel #2)
Black Mould (Graphic novel #3)
The Furthest Station (Novella)
The Hanging Tree
Detective Stories (Graphic novel #4)
Cry Fox (Graphic novel #5)
Water Weed (Graphic novel #6)
Lies Sleeping
The October Man (Novella)
The Fey and the Furious (Graphic novel #8)
False Value

PART ONE

THE PETER GRANT STORIES

The Home Crowd Advantage

(*Notionally set between* Rivers of London *and* Moon Over Soho)

Introduction

Write something for the Olympics they said.

Do I have to? I asked.

Yes, they said, we're going to publish a special edition in 2012 and we want to capitalise on the fact that London is going to host the Olympics.

So that was me told.

Up till then I'd avoided setting the books in a specific year because of the Olympics. Books are written years before they're published, so I'd either have to guess at the likely outcomes of the events or write a story referencing them after the games had taken place and risk nobody giving a toss what happened when the book finally made its way onto a shelf. The Olympics—that's so 2012, Grandad!

So when tasked to write a short story which was specifically Olympian, my solution was to set a story built around the events of the 1948 London Games which were safely over. So, I did some research and came across the France vs USA basketball final and the little idea birdie went 'ping'.

I'd originally had the idea that *Rivers*, *Moon* and *Whispers Under Ground* were all set in 2011 but that meant *Broken Homes* would be set during 2012—the Olympic year. Which I wanted to avoid. My solution was to declare that the first three books were always set during 2012 and hope no one noticed.

So strictly speaking 'The Home Crowd Advantage' isn't canon—but I still think it's fun.

Thanks to the city's diversity, there will be supporters from every Olympic nation. Every athlete will have a home crowd.

—Gold Medallist Denise Lewis
during her speech in support
of the London 2012 bid.

We were a grumpy lot that summer of 2012. There's nothing the police like better than a good moan, but in the run-up to the Olympics the Met had raised its game to world beating levels. What with the pension thing, the fitness thing and the personnel cuts, we were feeling hard done by. And on top of that we had to handle Olympic security.

I say "we" but my role, unofficially handed down from the Commissioner's office, was to stay as far away from any Olympic venues as was consistent with my duties. I guess they were worried about property damage, what with Covent Garden burning down, the ambulance hijack, that business in Oxford Circus and the thing that happened in Kew that was totally not my fault.

When Nightingale was called north of the border to deal with an unspecified 'situation' in Aberdeen, I found myself rattling around the Folly, alone except for Molly—which is, believe me, much creepier than being alone by yourself. As a result, when the phone rang my response time was pretty much instantaneous.

'Folly,' I said and there was a short pause at the other end.

'This is CCC, I'm looking for ECB9,' said a female voice.

'We used to be ECB9,' I said. 'But now we're the SAU or SCD-fourteen.'

The operator sighed—the Met reorganises every three years or so—nobody can keep up. Not even the people who draw up the organisational flow charts.

'Whoever you are now,' she said. 'I have a job for you.'

That was a surprise. The Folly has always operated on an informal word-of-mouth basis. Usually, when a senior officer on the spot thinks they may have a 'situation' which might benefit from some 'specialist' assistance, they know to call us directly. As part of the Olympic readiness programme, I had responded to a request to define the Folly's operational parameters, to better facilitate a co-ordinated and timely response. But I never expected it to filter down to CCC.

'Are you sure?' I asked.

'You're the guys who do magic, right?' asked the operator. She sounded testy.

'Sort of,' I said.

'Then this is your shout,' she said. 'Green Lanes Shopping Park.'

The operator didn't tell me much beyond the fact that 'specialist' assistance was required and that it was sierra-grade, urgent. So, I put my Kojak light on the roof and 'made progress' down the Essex Road in an attempt to arrive there in the same geological epoch as I started out. Half an hour later I turned into the access road of the shopping park to be met by blue tape, flashing lights and knots of uniforms standing around and trying to work out how this would improve their overtime pay.

I parked up beside an ambulance that was idling with its back doors open. Inside, a man in a hard hat and high-vis jacket was having his hands bandaged by the paramedic. A tall, spare, athletic white woman with a beaky nose and skipper's tabs introduced herself as Sergeant Warwick. She didn't look that pleased to see me.

'Are you it?' she asked after looking me up and down.

'Yes, sarge,' I said. 'What were you hoping for?'

'To be honest,' she said, 'someone a bit less cheeky.'

* * *

Green Lanes Shopping Park used to be the location
of the famous Haringey Arena where, back in the old
days, they used to show everything from ice hockey
to the Moscow State Circus. Paul Robeson sang there
in 1949 and Billy Graham launched his first British
crusade. With a rich history like that there was nothing to be done except flatten it and replace it with a
shopping arcade designed in the who-the-fuck-cares
school of retail architecture. The result was a two-sto-
rey warehouse with a flat roof designed to maximise
floor space and nothing else. The corner unit was
occupied by a Costa Coffee, sandwiched between a
Fitness First and Dreams: Britain's Leading Bed Specialist.

At approximately quarter past two on this particular
day, a well-dressed IC1 male in his late sixties, possibly
older, entered the shop, approached the counter and
proceeded to shout at the members of staff, in what
they thought was probably French. The staff had been
given clear instructions on how to deal with such situations, although none of them could remember what
these were. Instead, one of them asked the man to
leave while a second called the police. It might have
been a winning strategy, if another customer, presumably impatient for his coffee, had not intervened to

remonstrate with the suspect—going so far as to grab the old man's arm.

'That's when fire came out his hands,' said Matilda Stümpel, student and part-time barista. 'His hands didn't catch fire,' she gave Sergeant Warwick a poisonous look. 'It was like a ball of fire, okay?' She nodded at me. 'He believes me,' she said to Warwick, which was true.

'Can I see your phone?' I asked her.

She was reluctant to give it up but handed it over. 'It's stopped working anyway,' she said.

I cracked it open and wasn't surprised to find that the phone's chipset had been reduced to a fine, brownish powder.

'That was brand new,' said Matilda Stümpel, as I dropped the phone, and as much of the powder as I could catch, into an evidence bag. 'Am I going to get that back?'

I told her it was unlikely.

I didn't bother with the guy who had his hands burnt, Warwick had his details and the paramedic wanted to take him to casualty. So, I went off to meet the two uniforms who'd attended the scene first.

'So, you arrived on the scene?' I asked.

'That's right,' said the large talkative one. His colleague was small, balding but with unusually big hands with which he gestured, rather than talking.

'You went into the coffee shop and approached the suspect?'

'The way you do,' said the talkative one while his colleague nodded agreement.

'And then you turned round and left the premises?'

'That's right.'

'Any particular reason?'

'We thought,' said the talkative one, 'that it was time for a break.' His colleague made a palms-up gesture as if to say—what can you do?

'Did you just decide that, or did the suspect say something first?'

'He said we should go and get a cup of coffee,' said the talkative one while his partner mimed drinking from a cup with a saucer.

'So, you left?'

'Right.'

'To get some coffee?'

'Right.'

'Despite the fact that you were already in a coffee shop?'

The quiet one slowly shook his head at my inability to grasp the obvious. 'We had to,' he said in surprisingly deep baritone. 'All the baristas had run outside.'

'It's like hypnotism,' I told Warwick, after the two had been dispatched off to drink more coffee. But Warwick wasn't buying.

'Hypnotism doesn't work like that,' she said.

'And that's the way it's not like hypnotism,' I said.

'He's definitely on his own in there?'

'Everyone in the shop has been accounted for,' said Warwick.

'I'd better go get him, then,' I said.

'Are you sure you want to do that?'

'It's that or we call in CO19 and have them shoot him.'

'Don't be stupid, that's out of the question. I couldn't possibly authorise that,' she said. 'CO19 are all on standby for the games. We'd never get them up here.'

* * *

Your Metvest comes in the two basic flavours, the one with a plain white cover for wearing under your jacket and the one you get when you pass out of Hendon which is blue, has POLICE in nice reflective letters, front and back, and lots of useful pockets and clips. Strictly speaking, now that I'm plainclothes I should have traded that one in for the plain cover, but it's often useful when you're on a job to look as much like a copper as possible. So, I keep it in the emergency bag in the back of my Ford Asbo, along with other bits of kit from my uniform days, plus a couple of things I've added especially for 'special' jobs.

I put on the duty belt and taser as well and loaded up with all the kit I had in the bag. I didn't think I was going to need my notebook or the airwave radio, but members of the public are so used to us waddling around like Batman's fat younger brother that they often don't register what we are carrying—that can be useful.

'I've called for another ambulance,' said Warwick. 'Just to be on the safe side.'

There's a comfort, I thought, and started the long walk across the strip of car park to the front of the Costa Coffee. Once the initial excitement of transgression has faded, people are often keen to see a return to order. That's why they like to see a uniformed police officer. Even the criminals. And sometimes,—if things have escalated out of control and you're looking at somebody's dear old mum down the other end of your shotgun and two to six years with good behaviour is ratchetting up to life with a recommendation of thirty years minimum and your face on the front cover of a tabloid—especially the criminals.

That's when the uniform comes in handy. That and the ability to walk towards an incident projecting an air of quiet confidence and blokey no nonsense don't-worry-there's-nothing-we-can't-sort-out-ness, when what you really want to do is hide behind a riot shield.

After all that, the suspect wasn't even visible when I arrived at the shop doorway. There was only the one room, tables on the left, nooks and sofas on the right. A couple of chairs had gone over in the customers' scramble for the exit and I could smell coffee soaking into the carpet. My mum hates coffee stains. She says you never get them out, not even with the industrial strength solvent she buys under the counter at the cleaning wholesaler.

I stepped slowly into the shop.

'Hello, police,' I said loudly, 'Is there anyone in here?'

'Your friends are probably waiting for you outside,' said a voice from behind the counter. 'Why don't you go join them?'

Since I became an apprentice, everybody—and I mean everybody—with the slightest bit of magical potential in London has tried to put the glamour on me. I've built up an immunity.

'That's not going to work,' I said. 'Sorry.'

'Merde,' said the voice. 'In that case would you like a cup of coffee?'

'Yes please,' I said.

'So would I,' said the voice. 'Do you know how to work one of these machines?'

'I'll give it a go,' I said. 'I'm going to walk around the counter now—if that's okay with you?'

'If you can make a cup of coffee you can do what you like.'

I walked slowly and non-threateningly around the counter and got my first look.

13

He was sitting on the floor with his back against the wall, out of the line of sight for any possible sniper, but with a good view of the sides should someone try to flank him. Short, I thought, although it was hard to tell with him sitting down. Definitely seventies plus with thin grey hair cut in a side parting, blue eyes and a narrow face that had avoided jowls by not having enough spare flesh to droop.

I introduced myself.

'Antonin Bobet,' said the man. 'Who trained you?'

'Nightingale,' I said.

'Thomas Nightingale?' said Antonin. 'He's not dead?'

'Not as far as I can tell,' I said. 'Do you know him?'

'Are you going to make me wait much longer for the coffee?' asked Antonin.

I've always preferred ye olde greasy spoon to chain coffee shops but my dad, who had largely misspent his youth in the espresso bars of Soho, made sure I knew how to use a moka pot and the principles are the same as on the big commercial coffee machines—sort of.

Antonin, I noticed, shuffled sideways to stay out of convenient lunging range and was careful to keep an eye on me as I made two espressos.

'Both of them without milk,' said Antonin, as I reached for the steam nozzle.

I asked if he wanted sugar, but he declined and instructed me to sit on the floor with my back to the counter and place his coffee on the floor between us.

'Using only your left hand,' he said.

More than a metre separated us and I had to stretch awkwardly to place the cup within his reach. I also managed to spill half my own coffee and spent an entertaining minute or so wiping it off my Metvest and duty belt.

Antonin waited politely for me to finish rearranging myself before sipping his coffee.

'Not bad,' he said.

I sipped mine. The longer people sit around being calm and civilised, the harder it is for them to become uncivilised later—it's just too much effort. The rule of thumb is that if you keep them talking for over twenty minutes you can usually walk away without the use of force. Usually.

'Who trained you?' I asked.

'Maurice Guillaume,' he said. 'Not that you know him of course.'

'He was your master?'

This amused Antonin.

'How archaic,' he said. 'Maurice was my professeur at the Academy. Do you call Nightingale "master"?'

'Not if I can help it,' I said.

'Why not?'

'Too much history,' I said.

Antonin nodded.

'That I can understand,' he said, but I doubted it.

'Well Monsieur Bobet,' I said. 'Let's talk about how we get out of this situation.'

'Do you think Nightingale will be here soon?'

'He's out of the city,' I said. 'Is it important?'

'I killed a man,' said Antonin. 'On this very spot, I think, or at least quite close to here. I did it in 1948 so I think Nightingale may be a little more interested in the case than you. History, you understand.'

'I'm interested in history,' I said. 'Why don't you tell me what happened.'

'Why would a young man like you be interested in history?'

'So I can avoid repeating it.'

'Then stay away from men who talk about the Fatherland,' he said. 'That's my advice.'

'Good advice.'

'How far out of the city is Nightingale?' he asked.

I shrugged and offered to make another coffee.

'You can stay where you are,' he said. 'And I'll tell you a story.'

They do things differently in France, apparently, even in the wacky way-back days of the Third Republic. Antonin Bobet was from an old family in Lyon and had been selected, aged fourteen, to attend the Academy in Paris where he learnt the forms and wisdoms.

'In Latin?' I had to ask.

'The forms, yes,' said Antonin. 'The wisdoms were all in French.'

And it was all properly exam based and meritocratic and if certain old family names, like Bobet for example, turned up with unusual frequency in the rolls, then that was merely an assurance that quality and tradition were being maintained.

'Some of us valued our traditions,' said Antonin. 'Others wanted to be modern.'

'What about your Professor?' I asked.

'He was a Parisian,' he said. 'You can never be sure what Parisians believe in—beyond Paris of course.'

It was all a lot like the Folly as far as I could tell, including the point where it all came crashing down in 1940. Not that everyone thought the fall of the Third Republic was a bad thing—even if it had taken a German invasion to do it.

'After the Armistice we all made our choices,' said Antonin. 'I chose Petain and Professeur Guillaume chose De Gaulle.'

Antonin didn't elaborate as to his days working for the collaborationist Vichy Government except to claim, unprompted, that somebody had to ensure some continuity to ensure that the French state survived the war. Which it did in no small part, according to Antonin, thanks to the efforts of someone called Jean Bichelonne and people like Antonin.

'Not that any of this mattered to the Gaullists and Communists,' said Antonin. The resistance took a perversely dim view of collaborators and things might have gone very badly for him after the war if not for the timely intervention of his old professor. 'He said that purging me would be a waste of material.'

Which was why, in the summer of 1948, when Professor Guillaume told him they were travelling to London in 'support' of the French Olympic team, Antonin didn't ask what on earth kind of 'support' they were supposed to provide.

'You know what the terrible thing about the English is?' asked Antonin. 'You never do what is expected of you. Your city was in ruins, your people barely had enough to eat, your government was bankrupt and you think it's a good idea to hold the Olympics—unbelievable.' So Antonin had not been expecting much in the way of hospitality and he wasn't disappointed.

'And I'm not even going to talk about the food,' he said.

'Thank you for not bringing that up,' I said and he gave me a sharp look.

Professor Guillaume's plan was to 'help' the French basketball team to victory.

'How was he going to do that?' I asked.

'He was going to make their opponent's feet heavy,' said Antonin. He didn't know the details of the spell because he had strictly been the lookout man and, if necessary, the getaway driver. They had made their preparations and were about to leave for the first game— France versus Iran—when they received a visitor at their hotel.

'It was your 'master',' said Antonin. 'Nightingale.'

'And he warned you off?'

Antonin made a puffing noise. 'Nothing so obvious or indiscreet. He merely welcomed us to London and hoped that we would enjoy the games in the spirit of fraternal brotherhood and fair play that were the true Olympic ideals.'

'So he warned you off?'

'He warned us off.' And they stayed warned off because Nightingale was famous by that point as the most dangerous wizard in Europe. This did not sit well with Professor Guillaume, but what could they do? Things probably would have been left that way had not the French basketball team, buoyed up by emergency meat supplies from the Fatherland, managed to fight their way to the semi-finals where they beat Brazil 45 to 33 to face the Americans in the final.

This was too much for Professor Guillaume who resented the Americans almost as much as he resented the English. They knew that the Folly had been deci-mated at Ettersberg, so they decided to take a chance that Nightingale would be otherwise engaged and sneak into the Haringey Arena to carry out their original plan.

The arena had originally been built as an ice hockey rink and so they set up in the machine room. It was there, amongst the pipes and compressors, that Antonin had his change of heart.

'I said that I didn't think what we were doing was right. The Americans had been our allies and this was a violation of the Olympic spirit,' said Antonin. Professor Guillaume didn't take this well.

'He said he should have expected as much from a collaborationist like me and that I should have had my head shaved like the German-loving whore I was,' said Antonin. 'I told him that I didn't think it was right to be so petty to our allies and that it was unsportsmanlike. This he found very funny. "Unsportsmanlike," he shouted. "This is for France, what does France care for sportsmanlike?" He raised his hand to me.' Antonin shook his head. 'So I struck him with the pushing spell—I don't know what you call it in English—and down he went.'

And never got up again, on account of having smacked his head against a pipe on the way down. Antonin quickly determined that his Professor was permanently dead and then considered his next move.

'Letting France lose at basketball was one thing,' he said. 'Having her and the Academy disgraced by a murder investigation and trial was something else entirely.'

Antonin used a spell, ironically taught to him by Professor Guillaume, to bury the poor man around the back of the arena and then caught the first boat-train back to Paris. When he reported in, he was told that the mission had been unauthorised and that he had saved the French state an inquiry.

'Just like that?' I asked.

'Just like that,' said Antonin. Although it was made clear that it might be wise for him to take up a quiet life in the provinces somewhere. 'I went back to my family in Lyon,' he said.

Because I knew Nightingale would want to know, I made sure I asked what had happened to the Academy.

'They made the wrong choice after the Algerian Referendum,' he said. And consequently they were re-organised out of existence in 1965.

'So why are you here?' I asked.

'Apart from the coffee?' asked Antonin. 'I did a wrong thing sixty years ago and I thought it would be right to give Nightingale the chance to arrest me.'

That explained his overt use of magic in the coffee shop—he was looking to attract Nightingale's attention.

'You could have phoned ahead,' I said. 'We would have met you at the station.'

'I felt it was fitting that we met here at the scene of the

crime,' said Antonin. 'Man against man, magic against magic—the way they used to settle things in the old days.'

'Wait,' I said. 'Are we talking about a duel—a magic duel?'

'Of course,' said Antonin. 'Better than dying in hospital—no?'

Oh great, I thought, suicide by cop.

'I don't see why you have to wait for Nightingale,' I said. 'I'm perfectly capable of upholding the honour of my country.'

'Please,' said Antonin. 'You're still a boy.'

'I think that was an insult,' I said. 'At the very least I think I'm going to have to make you prove that you're worth Nightingale's time.'

'If you insist,' said Antonin.

'Are there rules?'

'No gods, no staffs, first man to stay down for the count loses and we suspend the contest if the building collapses.'

I took a deep breath and prepared myself.

'Very well,' I said. 'On the count of three?'

'That seems reasonable,' said Antonin. 'Although we could still wait for Nightingale.'

'No, I don't want to miss the opening ceremony on TV,' I said. 'Ready?'

'Yes,' he said.

'One,' I said and shot him with the taser.

Like I said, people don't notice half the kit hanging off your Metvest and I'd placed it out of sight by my leg when I'd spilt my coffee. I had him cuffed before he stopped twitching, but in deference to his age I did it with his hands in front.

* * *

We ambulanced him back to UCH where Dr Walid stuck Antonin's head in the MRI and kept him lightly sedated while we waited for Nightingale to arrive. I'm getting quite good at interpreting the grey smudges as they appear on the screen, and I've got to say it didn't look good for Antonin Bobet.

'Hyperthaumaturgical Necrosis,' said Dr Walid. 'He wouldn't have lasted long—you definitely saved his life.'

'Fair play,' he spat at me when I brought him lunch. 'You call electrocuting me fair play?'

I didn't bother to answer that, but I did apologise for the quality of the food.

Nightingale returned and spent a morning chatting while I caught up with the paperwork and squared the incident with Haringey Borough Command. I made a point of calling Sergeant Warwick personally to thank her for her help—always useful to build contacts.

A very polite man from the French Embassy turned

up that afternoon, shook our hands and assured us that if we could see our way to allowing the French Government to repatriate their wayward son, they would consider it a great favour.

'We only have his word for it that he killed Professor Guillaume and I'm not sure what purpose would be served by excavating Green Park Shopping Centre,' said Nightingale. 'And it's not as if he has much time left.'

So we put the question to Antonin, who chose repatriation.

'At least the food will be better,' he said and I couldn't argue with that.

The Domestic

(Set between Moon Over Soho *and*
Whispers Under Ground)

Introduction

Waterstones liked the idea of having a special edition with a short story so much they asked for one to include in an exclusive edition of *Whispers Under Ground*. I'd always avoided short stories before, they're a lot of work for a minimum word count and hard to sell. But writing 'The Home Crowd Advantage' had whet my appetite, so I agreed. I wanted something anchored in the hum-drum, the everyday and in a situation that confronts police on a daily basis.

The tricky thing about architectural fashion is that it's never as demarcated as the textbooks make out. The terrace mid-way up Prince of Wales Road was doing its best to pretend it was Regency, but the sash windows, slapdash stucco and half basement all said mid-Victorian at the earliest. I gave it the once over. The paint was grubby rather than dirty and the iron railings had been maintained free of rust. First wave right-to-buy property owner, I thought, from back in the days when Camden Council still had terrace flat conversions on its books.

My domestic lived down a flight of external stairs, in the basement flat. The front door was trapped in an alcove under the steps to what would have originally been the main entrance before the house was subdivided— the better for the unspeakably common tradesman to come and go as unobtrusively as possible. The doorbell chimed when I pressed it and habit made me step out of the confined alcove while I waited for it to open. It's always good to have some space to manoeuvre when the door opens—just in case.

When it did open, a little old white woman stuck her head round the doorjamb and peered at me suspiciously.

'Yes,' she said. 'Can I help you?'

'Mrs Eugenia Fellaman?' I asked.

'Yes,' she said.

'My name's Peter Grant. I'm a police officer and I wondered if I might come in and have a quick word.' I showed her my warrant card—she wasn't impressed.

'I've already spoke to the other one,' she said.

'Yes Ma'am I know,' I said. The 'other one' being Sergeant Bill Crosslake who had called me in. 'He asked me to talk to you. He thought I might be able to help.'

She stepped out of her front door the better to chase me back up to street level.

'Well he thought wrong,' she said, and as she came into the daylight I saw the faded purple of a bruise on her left cheek.

'Can I ask how you got that bruise?'

I watched as she carefully didn't lift her hand to her face.

'I walked into the door, didn't I?' she said. 'You get like that when you're a bit older.'

'We both know that's not true,' I said.

She folded her arms. She was wearing a green woollen loose knit jumper, clean but with frayed cuffs. Her hair was grey, thinning and gathered back into a ponytail. There were a pair of red framed reading glasses hung around her neck on black beaded cord. She had grey eyes and a good line in belligerent defiance.

'It was them upstairs that called you in,' she said. 'Wasn't it?'

Actually, it had been the couple upstairs, but also the Romanian students next door and a member of the public who'd happened to be walking his dog outside. All had dialled 999 within five minutes of each other, which prompted an India-Grade response from the area car, who arrived within three minutes. When the responding officers talked their way inside the flat, they found Mrs Fellaman, definite signs of a struggle but no trace of another person or persons on the premises.

Mrs Fellaman claimed that she was completely alone and that she'd merely fallen against the chair, which had broken, causing her to reach out in an involuntary fashion, and pull down a row of ceramic elephants and an antique ormolu clock.

Violent crime, like charity, begins at home. Twenty percent of all murders occur in the victim's residence and forty percent of all female murder victims are killed by their partner. Which is why the responding officers gently, but firmly, insisted on searching the flat. They found nobody and Mrs Fellaman, with a certain amount of satisfaction, sent them on their way.

'We're concerned about your safety,' I said.

'That's nice,' she said. 'But it's my patience you should be worried about. That other one, the big one, has been round here two times already and he never found nothing either.'

The Camden response team had passed the details onto the local neighbourhood safety team which was headed by Sergeant Crosslake. He'd talked to the neighbours and confirmed their stories, made a follow up visit to Mrs Fellaman, found nothing and in frustration sat outside, in his own car, on his own time, the next evening until he heard the argument for himself.

'That was proper rowing,' he'd told me. 'And there were definitely two voices.'

But again, when he'd talked himself inside, there was just Mrs Fellaman entirely on her own.

'And there was something else,' Crosslake had said. 'There was something off about that flat.'

'Third time lucky,' I told Mrs Fellaman.

'With all this crime around,' she said. 'I don't know why you bother.'

Because when we're not ticking boxes and achieving performance targets going forward, we actually try to prevent the occasional crime. Not to mention that 'Granny beaten to death after police visited three times—shocker!' is not the sort of headline you want hanging over your conscience, let alone your career.

'It's no bother,' I said.

'It is to me,' she said. 'And I'm sick and tired of it. Have you got a warrant?'

I admitted that I did not.

'Then you can piss off,' she said, and locked herself back inside.

Crosslake had said something was off about the flat.

'Your kind of weird bollocks,' he'd told me. 'That's why I called you in.'

Crosslake was career uniform and had been doing neighbourhood policing since back in the days when it was just called "policing". He didn't have "instincts", he had thirty years of experience—which was much more reliable.

There was no way I was going to get a warrant because part of the Folly's arrangement with the rest of the criminal justice system is that we don't bother them with the weird shit and in return they occasionally look the other way when the weird shit happens. But if I was going to barge into Mrs Fellaman's flat then I'd better make sure that there was actually some weird shit going on so that they could ignore it.

This was a job for Toby the Wonder Dog.

* * *

I don't know whether it was because he was exposed to

magic during the Punchinello case or whether all dogs, particularly small yappy ones, have an instinct for the uncanny, but I've always found Toby a pretty reliable magic detector. I've actually done controlled laboratory experiments that indicate that he can detect magical activity up to ten metres away, although false positives can be generated by cats, other dogs and the remote possibility of a sausage.

That's why I fed him a sausage before we started the stakeout, although that did mean I had to keep the car window open. I parked outside the flat at seven in the evening and settled in. Toby curled up on the passenger seat with his feet twitching, intermittently nudging me on the thigh, and presumably dreaming of squirrels while I cracked open Juvenal and laboured through the last part of Book III: Flattering Your Patron Is Hard Work. It had been my set text for months and had led me to think of the Romans as a bunch of Bernard Manning wannabes with an empire. At nine fifteen Toby woke up with a start and stared about suspiciously—I put down my Latin homework. Was it going to be police work or sausage, I wondered?

Toby's head stopped swinging with his nose pointed directly at Mrs Fellaman's flat and he started to bark, the proper watchdog bark which was what got those original wolves invited in to share the fire in the first place. Not a sausage then.

I left Toby in the car and slipped down the iron stairs to the basement. I stopped at the door and listened. A raised voice, definitely Mrs Fellaman's although I couldn't make out the words. Then a response, younger, deeper, male. Then a crash of breaking crockery.

I banged on the door and called Mrs Fellaman's name.

'It's the police,' I shouted. 'Open up.'

It went silent inside.

'You might as well let me in Mrs Fellaman,' I called. 'I know you've got a ghost in there.'

Toby stopped barking. The door opened.

'What do you know about it?' asked Mrs Fellaman.

'I have reason to believe that you are consorting with a spirit in contravention of the Act against Conjuration, Witchcraft and Dealing with Evil and Wicked Spirits 1604,' I said. The Witchcraft Act had actually been superseded in 1736 but I find quoting it helps break the ice on the doorstep.

'No I ain't,' said Mrs Fellaman. 'And in any case he ain't wicked, he's my husband.'

I waited until she'd figured out what she'd just said.

'Bugger,' she said, and sighed. 'You'd better come in.'

I followed her into a mean little corridor which opened into a mean little living room/kitchen combination. She'd done her best, but the whole terrace had been built cheaply and the basement had been where the Victorians had stuck the kitchen, the servants and

33

the coal bunker. Nothing could disguise the low ceiling and permanently moist walls. I doubted it got a lot of sunshine either.

'I'd offer you a cup of tea,' said Mrs Fellaman. 'But I don't think I've got any cups left.'

There was a scatter of broken pottery spread across the floor.

I suggested that we sit down at the kitchen table, but she insisted that she wanted to sweep up first. I sat and let her bustle about—I wanted her relaxed and talkative. From under the sink she produced a white enamel camping mug and the kind of plastic cup that comes as the top bit of a thermos. So she made tea after all and, even better, offered me a custard cream. It's hard for even the most hardened criminal to maintain a belligerent tone with someone who's eating a custard cream biscuit. Although I suppose a chocolate digestive might do in a pinch.

Once she had a cup of tea in her own hand I asked her whether she was sure the ghost was her husband.

'Of course I am,' she said. 'I knew him as soon as he appeared.'

'And when did he appear?' I asked.

Three months earlier, she told me vaguely, but I pinned her down to a specific date and made a note. You never know when precise information will come in handy.

'So the ghost of your husband appears,' I said. 'And you decide to have an argument with him.'

'I didn't decide,' she said. 'We always used to row, you know, some people you just row with—I suppose even him being passed on couldn't change that.'

'Did he hit you?'

'Don't be stupid. How could he hit me?' asked Mrs Fellaman. 'He's a ghost.'

'So how did you get the bruises then?'

'I was a clot and ran into the wall,' she said.

'How did you manage to do that?'

Mrs Fellaman looked sheepish. 'I forgot he was a ghost and he made me so angry—.' She made punching motions with her right hand. 'I ran right through him. Hit the wall, fell over. You know how it is, you grab the nearest thing and that was the cupboard and that fell over and the next thing I know I've got the Old Bill knocking on my door.'

'And what happened tonight,' I pointed at the smashed cups with my pen.

'I was throwing them at him,' said Mrs Fellaman. 'Well he makes me so cross, he always did. It was his fault, he was always so stubborn.' She gave me a defiant look.

I decided to see if we could have a word with "Mr Fellaman".

'What was your husband's name Mrs Fellaman?' I asked even though I already knew.

'His name was Victor,' she said. 'His parents were a bit la-di-dah.'

'Can you summon him for me?'

'You're joking,' she said. 'He comes and goes when he wants—always did.'

I knew how to get a ghost's attention, although I'd been hoping to get through the case without doing anything too overt. Still Mrs Fellaman had been consorting with a ghost for at least three months so I doubted I could shock her any further.

I conjured a werelight and stuck it to the centre of the kitchen table.

Mrs Fellaman's eyes were round. 'What's that?' she asked.

'Ghost-nip,' I said. 'This should bring your husband out.'

Normally when you feed a ghost, they drain the magic quite gently and the werelight dims slowly, but this time the ball of light darkened to a dim crimson almost instantly. I looked around quickly and found the ghost, standing by the side wall, staring at me in apparent amazement.

He was young, early twenties, wearing a rather nice suit with a slim shirt with a button-down collar. In the 1950s it was called the City Gent look and my dad probably had a suit like that - at least until my Mum got the keys to his wardrobe. That was a Mod suit.

'He's a bit young isn't he?' I asked.

'He looks just like he did when I met him,' she said. 'There's no reason for him to look old, is there?'

Except generally speaking all the ghosts I'd met looked the age they did when they died. Lesley says to always check the shoes, so I did—they were old, worn, too big for his feet and an unpleasant brown colour. No Mod would have been seen dead in those shoes.

'Hello Victor,' I said. The ghost looked at me blankly.

'Talk to him, Victor,' hissed Mrs Fellaman. 'He's a policeman.'

'What do you want?' asked the ghost. His accent was wrong too, not sixties cockney but older—I recognised it. He wasn't what he seemed, and I didn't want to prolong the conversation and feed him magic for much longer.

'What's you mum's name?' I asked.

The ghost hesitated. 'What do you want to know for?'

'No reason,' I said. The hesitation had told me all I needed to know. I shut down the werelight and the ghost went suddenly transparent.

'Martha,' said the ghost in a whisper and then he was gone.

'Bring him back,' said Mrs Fellaman.

'Was Martha the name of his mother?' I asked.

Mrs Fellaman shook her head.

'He didn't know the answer, did he?'

'Well he's dead,' she said. 'You're bound to forget stuff once you're dead.'

'That's true,' I said, and it was. Most of the ghosts I've met always give the impression that they aren't all there mentally. My theory is that they are echoes, near-sentient imprints in the stone and concrete around them. But that's just a theory.

'See,' she said.

'But the thing is, Eugenia,' I said, 'before I knocked on the door I requested what's known as an intelligence package on you and it turns out your husband left you thirty years ago and is currently living in Prestatyn, Wales with a woman called Blodwyn.'

'I knew that,' said Mrs Fellaman. 'I'd just assumed that he'd died recently, left the Welsh bint to her own devices and come back home where he belonged.'

'I had the local police call round,' I said. 'He's alive and well.'

'Pity,' she said, and slumped in her chair.

I told her to stay put while I fetched some more equipment from my car, but she barely acknowledged me. Toby was pleased to see me and I gave him the requisite amount of encouragement for being a good boy. Grabbed the little and the big hammers from the boot and went back down to see how Mrs Fellaman was doing.

She was still slumped in her chair.

'So, who have I been talking to?' she asked.

'Definitely a ghost,' I said. 'Just not your husband.' Victorian terraces were pretty much all built with similar design features and if you know any architectural history at all it's fairly easy to spot when something is missing. Like the pantry alcove that should have been to the left of the bricked-up fireplace, very close to where the ghost had materialised—I did not think that was a coincidence.

Mrs Fellaman sighed. 'He did look like my Victor.'

'I believe you,' I said. 'He must have changed his appearance to suit you.'

'How would he know?'

'Good question,' I said and banged the small hammer on the wall until I got a hollow noise. I swapped for the big hammer. 'I'm afraid I'm about to make a bit of a mess,' I said, and got a good two-handed grip on the long shaft.

'Wait a minute,' said Mrs Fellaman.

It was an awkward swing, what with the low ceiling, but the iron head of the hammer went through on the first blow. I knocked out the loose plaster around the edges, got out my key-ring torch and had a look. As I did, I got a strong flash of carbolic soap and fish guts, the smell of sweat and a blast of cold that made my fingers numb. The vestigia pretty much confirmed my suspicions and so I wasn't nearly so surprised as I might have been when the beam of the key-ring torch fell upon the empty eye socket of a skull. I swept the light around and thought I could make out the rest of a skeleton collapsed at the bottom of the void.

I told Mrs Fellaman that she would need to find somewhere to stay for the next couple of days.

'Whatever for?' she asked.

'Because I'm about to call my colleagues at the Major Investigation Team, tell them that I've found a body and they're going to be round here mob handed to investigate,' I said.

'What kind of body?' asked Mrs Fellaman.

One that I suspect was walled up, judging from the shoes, in the late 19th Century. Some domestic worker whose employer got a bit heavy handed one day—one of those little Victorian stories that didn't get talked about. I looked at Mrs Fellaman who was staring morosely around her kitchen/living room area. Or perhaps there was somebody else after the first Mr Fellaman decamped to the Welsh seaside. She obviously had a temper did our Eugenia. As I said—crime often begins at home.

Fortunately, that question was not my responsibility. Nine times out of ten, once the bones were gone, so was the ghost. Although I thought I might take Toby for walkies past the house for the next couple of weeks— just to be on the safe side. I turned on my phone and keyed up Belgravia.

'I don't suppose you'd just consider leaving him in place, would you?' asked Mrs Fellaman.

'What for?' I asked.

'I rather liked the company,' she said.

The Cockpit

(Set between Whispers Under Ground
and Broken Homes)*

Introduction

So Waterstones now expected a bloody short story with every book and I was beginning to get the hang of the short form. I thought it might be fun to actually set a story in the branch of Waterstones I used to work in. This also allowed me to insert a Ghostbusters joke which, if nobody else got it, at least gave me a great deal of pleasure.

'It's not easy being a bookseller,' said Warwick Anderson—bookseller. 'Especially in that branch. It's a listed building, so Waterstones can't put in a lift and we have to carry the stock up and down the stairs.'

'So, you were tired?' I said.

Warwick took a sip of his coffee. We were in a spare office that the company had made available to us at Waterstones' gigantic art deco store on Piccadilly. We were there because Warwick Anderson refused to go within five hundred metres of his old store in Covent Garden.

He was a white guy in his late twenties with slightly mad blonde hair flying up into spikes.

'Well, I already had to do the overnight on my own, so that didn't help,' said Warwick, because the perennial problem for all retailers the world over are the customers. Not only do they clutter up the shop, but they also demand to be reminded of the title of a book they read a review about in the Telegraph, given directions to The Lion King, helped to find a book their mum will like and, occasionally, purchase some actual merchandise. All of this customer-facing activity gets in the way of the shelving, merchandising, stickering, destickering, table pyramiding and stock returning that is necessary for the smooth operation of a modern bookshop. The bigger stores can have whole shifts devoted to coming in early and making sure their shelves are ship shape, but small stores have to resort to the occasional overnighter.

'You can get a tremendous amount of work done if there are no customers in the way,' said Warwick. 'It's crucial if you have to move a section or something.'

'And you were on your own?' asked Lesley.

'Yes,' said Warwick, who was obviously disturbed by Lesley's face mask. 'Peggy had been with me the night before, but last night it was just me.'

Lesley checked her notebook. 'This would be Peggy Loughliner?' she said.

'That's right,' said Warwick, looking anywhere but at Lesley's face. 'I was in the basement shifting celebrity chefs from one end of the cookery section to the other when a book hit me in the back.'

Warwick had spun around, but found he was still alone. There was a book at his feet. It was Banksy's Wall and Piece. Fortunately, it was the paperback version.

'Or else that would have really hurt,' said Warwick.

Spooked, he'd taken the time to check the rest of the shop, including the staff areas and the three entry points, but didn't find any evidence that he wasn't alone. He went back to his shelving and was more annoyed than frightened when he was hit on the back of the head by a soft toy—the kind on offer at the till point. He was just about to whirl around and catch the perpetrator red handed when approximately five shelves of the art section hit him in the back—including two display shelves of Art Monographs.

'It's not funny,' said Warwick. 'Some of those Taschen books are huge.'

Actually, the CCTV footage was sort of funny, in a cruel YouTube kind of way. Unfortunately, the camera had been positioned to cover a blind spot behind the till, so the books were already in mid-flight before they appeared on screen. Warwick was just visible on the left of frame being knocked down by the sheer weight of literature. Worse than that, a couple had struck him squarely on the back of the head, rendering him semi-conscious.

He'd managed to stagger to the phone at the downstairs till and dial 999 before collapsing. The response team had been forced to break in, adding to the damage. And, having waved Warwick off in the ambulance, they called in the store manager to take care of the door before being called away to deal with a birthday party that was explosively decompressing outside the newly rebuilt Genius Bar in the piazza.

A DS from the CW's PSU, that's the Charing Cross Primary Crime Unit to you, evaluated the case and, since Warwick had suffered only a minor concussion, there didn't seem to have been a break-in prior to the arrival of the police, and nothing appeared to have been stolen, assigned it to his most junior PC with strong hints that it should be cleared, dumped or passed into oblivion by the end of the day. The PC, who shall remain forever nameless, had been at CW with both me and Lesley and had been following our subsequent careers with the same appalled interest engendered by the early round contestants in Britain's Got Talent, so he decided this was just the sort of weird shit that the Special Assessment Unit, aka the Folly, aka those weirdos, had been formed to deal with.

'You know what I reckon,' said Warwick Anderson. 'I reckon it was a poltergeist.'

I don't have time to talk about the nature of ghosts here, but let's just say that like the mentally ill, they almost never pose a danger to the public. And when they do it hardly ever involves throwing physical objects about. However, according to Nightingale, when they do start flinging the furniture it can be very serious. So I arranged for us to spend the night in the, possibly, haunted bookshop.

'And I have to be here because?' asked Lesley.

'So there's corroboration if anything happens,' I said.

'And Toby?' she asked.

'To wake us up if anything happens,' I said.

The shop manager, a short, round and strangely asymmetrical white man in his mid-thirties also wanted to know about the dog.

'Don't worry,' I said. 'He's specially trained.'

'Oh, he's special all right,' said Lesley.

The Covent Garden branch of Waterstones had been created by purchasing three shops — one medium sized one on New Row and two small ones on Garrick Street — and then knocking them together and fitting out the basement. This gave it three entrances, four till points and a very odd shape. Lots of dead space, I noticed, ideal for shoplifting.

I asked the manager about it, and he said I'd be surprised by what got stolen.

'Poetry mainly,' he said.

'Really?' I asked.

'Really,' he said.

I supposed that being right next to the Garrick Club they got a better class of shop lifter.

I'd noticed an interesting windowed dome over the main till on my first visit, but when I did a cursory historical and architectural search online that afternoon, I couldn't find any reference to it at all. I got the impression that the central section had once been a hall or a ballroom—somewhere built for display.

The manager would have preferred to have spent the night in the shop with us, but we suggested that if he were that worried he could always wait in his car outside—he declined.

Once he'd shown us how to lock up and set the alarm, in case we left early, and had a strained telephone conversation with his cluster manager, he departed with many a worried backward glance.

The ground floor was an L-shaped space made up of obviously quite a large hall, the main entrance, and a similar sized section at an angle which contained the main till with the glazed dome above it. The stock room and loading bay were behind the till and at the other end two smaller wings, children's books and travel, ended with doors out onto Garrick Street. A set of central stairs led down to the basement where Art, Self-Help, History, Politics and the ever-expanding Cookery section lay.

We did what we've come to call an Initial Vestigium Assessment or IVA—which consisted of me and Lesley wandering around the shop trying to sense if anything occult had happened inside. It wasn't easy, because books have the same effect on vestigia as those egg-box shaped bits of foam have on sound. It was a phenomena much commented on in the literature, or at least in the literature I'd managed to skim through that afternoon. Most practitioners cite the effect as the reason why it was much easier to have a nap in one of the Folly's libraries than in the smoking room where they were supposed to.

There was definitely something at the main till under the dome on the ground floor. A whiff of the slaughterhouse mingled with shouting, excitement, desire, disappointment and rotting straw. Downstairs, where the 'attack' had taken place, it was just your normal central London background of pain, joy, sweat, tears and the occasional inexplicable horse or sheep.

According to the literature there are basically two types of ghosts, those that only show themselves when people are present and those that only come out when nobody is there. There's Latin tags for both types but I can never remember what they are. So, the big question was whether to set up camp where the unfortunate Warwick Anderson was buried in books or to wait in the manager's office and monitor via CCTV. In the end we decided to wait in Art where the attack took place and if nothing happened after three hours move to the office—which was closer to the staff room and the coffee in any case.

'Hold on,' said Lesley as we settled into our chairs. 'Didn't the children's section used to be downstairs?'

'I don't remember getting called to a job here,' I said.

'I used to buy presents for my nieces and nephews,' she

said. 'And the children's section was there.' She pointed to a square alcove whose shelves were currently labelled Street Art, Interiors and Photography. Street Art being graffiti with a dollar value on the international market.

'At least that bit was where Harry Potter and Roald Dahl were,' she said. 'Although Tracy preferred Darren Shan to Harry Potter. I used to check the table for new stuff.'

The display table in the alcove was currently sporting a sign which read: Never Without Art, a category which appeared to consist of big glossy books with tastefully photographed white women on the front cover.

I rummaged around in the go-bag for the first of the snacks and Toby lay down on his back at our feet and stuck his legs in the air.

At least we had plenty to read.

In three hours I ate two packets of crisps, a ham sandwich and read sixty pages of Policing With Contempt by Victor Baker, the alleged pen name of a serving police officer in some force up north. Whoever he was, he really hated paperwork, political correctness and yearned for the simpler days of yore. I reckoned that if his skipper ever worked out who he was, he was going to get a close look at the good old days via the application of a telephone directory to the tender parts of his body.

We decided it was time for coffee and a possible shift to the manager's office.

I'd just put the kettle on when Toby started barking.

Me and Lesley looked at each other and then ran for the door. We would have made it back to the Art section faster if we hadn't tripped over each other's feet in the narrow corridor that ran past the manager's office. By the time we got there it was all over.

There were four neat stacks of books lined up in front of our chairs.

'Symmetrical book stacking,' I said. 'Just like the British Library in 1896.'

'You're right, Peter,' said Lesley. 'No human being would stack books like this.'

Having established that some sort of weird shit was going on, step two, in the as yet completely theoretical Modern Procedure Guide for Supernatural Police Officers, was to try and categorise what it is you're dealing with. With ghosts, the easiest way was to pump a bit of magic into them and see what form they take.

I conjured up a werelight which caused Toby to take refuge behind the till counter—he's a veteran of many of my practise sessions.

Shadows flickered amongst the shelves as the werelight dimmed and took on a crimson hue.

'Definitely something,' said Lesley.

'I can't see a figure,' I said.

Usually a ghost would have manifested by that stage.

'Give it some welly,' said Lesley.

I upped the intensity of the werelight until it practically gave off lens flare. Then suddenly it shrank down to a small sapphire blue star and winked out.

'Uh oh,' said Lesley and we both dived for the safety of the till counter just in time for the shop to explode.

Well, not explode exactly. As far as we could reconstruct it later fully half the books in the basement shot off their shelves and would have sailed across the shop if they hadn't met the books from the opposite shelves coming the other way, with a rattling sound of collision.

Strangely, some areas were untouched, not one Nigella Lawson book left its shelf but every single copy of Paulo Coelho's The Alchemist was found jammed into an air conditioning vent.

'What the fuck was that?' asked Lesley once the noise had died down.

'That didn't feel like a ghost,' I said.

Toby licked my face, which was disgusting, but there was no way I was sticking my head above the level of the till just yet.

Lesley cautiously took her hands off her head and risked a peep over the countertop. When nothing bad happened, I joined her.

'What did it feel like?' she asked.

It had felt a bit like the first time I'd met Mama Thames or when Beverley Brook kissed me, or the Old Man of the River had turned his gaze upon me. Like the smell of blood and the taste of Plasticine, liked crossed legs and chicken feathers.

'Definitely not a ghost,' I said. 'I want to check something.'

We tiptoed over the books on the floor and up the stairs, which were fortunately clear of books, although a display case full of Dan Brown's had been flung into the travel section.

A drift of brightly coloured volumes for toddlers and early readers stretched out from the Children's section towards the stairwell. I motioned Lesley towards the area under the dome.

'Tell me what you sense,' I said.

Even without her mask on it can be hard to tell what Lesley's thinking. The damage to her face had stripped it of the markers that we rely on to read the expressions of others. Still, I was getting better at interpreting what I did see and what she showed under the dome was puzzlement, then disgust and then recognition.

'Cock fighting ring,' she said.

'That's what I thought,' I said. 'All that excitement, activity and on top of that the power that gets released at the point of death.'

'Chicken ghost?' said Lesley. 'No, wait, you said it wasn't a ghost.'

'Do you know how gladiator fights got started?' I asked.

Lesley indicated that not only did she not know this interesting historical fact, but that she would like me to impart it sometime before old age and death.

'They started as part of a religious ceremony at grand Roman funerals,' I said.

'And you know this because?'

'Horrible Histories,' I said.

'So you're thinking what?'

I told her.

'You're kidding me,' she said.

'Okay,' I said. 'Say something bad about books.'

'What?'

'Say something disparaging about books and reading,' I said.

'Why me?' asked Lesley.

'Because it will be more convincing coming from you,' I said.

Lesley looked around self-consciously and then said: 'Nobody ever learnt anything from a book.'

I thought I heard a rustle downstairs—so did Lesley.

'Books are for losers,' she said.

Definitely movement, and it wasn't us. I checked and it wasn't Toby either.

'Oh my god,' said Lesley as we went downstairs.

'Exactly,' I said.

'Yeah, well don't sound so smug,' she said. 'Look at this place. It's a mess.'

'I have a plan for that,' I said and told her.

'Not me again,' she said.

'You've got a better voice,' I said.

Lesley agreed and, after a moment's thought, went upstairs to fetch a book from the Children's section. She waved it at me when she came back down.

'Harry Potter,' I said. 'Really?'

'Since I'm reading,' she said. 'It's my choice'

I created another werelight, a nice gentle one, and addressed the bookshop at large.

'Hello,' I said in my brightest voice. 'My name's Peter Grant and tonight we're going to play a game called 'put all the books back in order.' And if you're especially good and well behaved, my friend Lesley's going to read you a story.'

* * *

Lesley, the coward, claimed she had a medical appointment and left me to explain it to the manager the next morning.

'There's a god living in my branch,' said the manager when I was finished.

'A Genius Loci,' I said. 'A spirit of place. And it's more accurate to say that it is the shop—in a metaphysical sense. A god or goddess of books and reading.'

'But why here?' he asked plaintively.

'Well, it's a book shop,' I said.

'So what?' asked the manager. 'My last branch didn't have a local god in it. None of the other managers have ever mentioned anything like this—I'm sure I would have remembered. Why here?'

Because, I thought, the cockfighting ring on your top floor provided a reservoir of vestigia which interacted with all those young minds reading books downstairs, and a spirit of place formed like a pearl around a bit of grit. Only I wasn't going to tell him that. Because not only couldn't I prove any of it, it was also a bloody dreadful simile.

Then the children's section had been moved upstairs and the poor little deity started to feel unloved.

'Just one of those things,' I said.

'But what am I supposed to do about it,' he asked. 'Sacrifice a goat?'

'About once a week somebody has to sit down and read it a book,' I said.

'What kind of book?'

'It's not the book that's important,' I said. 'It's the reading.'

The Loneliness of the Long-Distance Granny

(Takes place just after Foxglove Summer)

Introduction

There's something haunting about a motorway service station at night, it might be the melancholy rumble and swish of traffic or that they exist as islands of fluorescent light amongst the rural darkness. Jasper Fforde used one as a metaphor for the transition between life and death and I'd be lying if I didn't have that, and the final story of Sapphire and Steel in my mind when I wrote this story.

I know it can be hard to keep track of all the characters in a long running series so to help out I'd like to remind you that not-Nicole is the human changeling child whose mum tried to send her back to Faerie.

There's something uniquely dangerous about a motorway services station in the dead hours of the night. You can feel it as you pull off the slip road and cruise through the sodium wastes of the empty car park to stop by the sad little strip of landscaping that separates the vehicles from the children's play area. You get out of the car to silence except for the washing machine rumble of passing traffic and usually something tinny and corporately approved echoing out of the main entrance.

You can have some seriously weird and melancholy thoughts at a motorway service station, about your mortality, about the doomed future of the human race and just who thinks it's justified to charge 10p over the odds for petrol. It's a bloody crime is what it is.

I try not to drive at night but if you do you've got to stop regularly or risk the chance of waking up with a face full of airbag. Therefore, the best thing is to get in and out of the service station as fast as possible - before the blues come creeping around your shoulder.

Ben Aaronovitch

Still, had I been alone I would have kept driving until I was safe in the embrace of the city, but I wasn't on my own.

'Sick,' said not-Nicole as we pulled up. Beverley jumped out, opened the passenger door and made sure not-Nicole got a good three metres from the Asbo before she threw up.

She hadn't eaten much in the last day or two, so it was mostly fluid. They don't have a lot in the way of chocolate, refined sugar or carbonated beverages in faerie land, so she'd gone a bit mad for her first seven days amongst people and then spent the last three days bringing it all back up.

While she did that, I did a fast scan of the car park. A couple of mid-range saloons, one Chelsea tractor and a Mercedes with its bonnet up. A white man leant over the engine calling instructions to another person in the driver's seat. I couldn't hear any engine noises, not even the starter, and the tone indicated that tempers were being lost. One part of my mind idly tagged them a potential problem and moved on.

Not-Nicole straightened up.

'You've got to be empty by now,' said Beverley who really had no sympathy at all.

'Water,' said not-Nicole

'What's the magic word?" asked Beverley.

'Water please,' said not-Nicole and Beverley rewarded her with a warm bottle of Evian.

'That was the last,' said Beverley. 'We need to stock up.'

The core of the service station was your standard one size fits all redbrick mini mall with a glass pyramid roofette in the middle and the aesthetic appeal of a rural bus shelter.

And like a bus shelter there were certain circumstances in which one was very glad to see it and its cornucopia of 24-hour shops and fast food outlets. While Beverley took not-Nicole to the toilets I hit WH Smith for bottled water and enough Haribo to get me safely back to London. The white girl behind the counter must have been dying of boredom because she perked up as soon as I walked in. She wanted to know where I was coming from.

'Herefordshire,' I said which led to an explanation as to why we were on the M4. In the fluorescent light her skin looked pale and unhealthy and there were smudges under her eyes. I remembered feeling as bad as she looked doing late shifts during my probation. She was wearing a badge that announced her name was Suzanne.

Just as Suzanne was half-heartedly trying to tempt me with a special offer on a bar of chocolate the size of a paperback book, a low moan sounded from the far side of the building. She froze and we both listened to see if it came again.

A glass smashed in the distance and there was the distinctive sound of stacked furniture falling over followed by swearing in a foreign language. Suzanne relaxed.

'It's just Cornel,' she said. 'The security guard.' And then, as if it explained everything, said, 'He's Romanian.'

I paid up and wished Suzanne good luck for the rest of the shift at which she smiled wanly. As I left the building there was another crash, a long moan in Romanian.

As I was walking back to the Asbo one of the white men by the stalled car attracted my attention.

'Excuse me, mate,' he called. 'Do you know anything about engines?'

As it happens I don't really, but I like to show willing and I wouldn't have joined the police if I didn't like sticking my nose in other people's business.

I changed course and started walking towards him.

'You having a problem, mate?' I asked, which is the correct ritual response in these situations.

'Yeah,' he said. 'Won't start.' He was smaller than me but stocky, middle aged with a long nose, deep set eyes and receding fair hair in a side parting. He bobbed nervously as I approached and ushered me towards the bonnet. The second man got out of the driver's seat and peered at me over the roof. He was younger, slimmer and had more hair but a similar cast to the nose and eyes made me think they might be related.

I saw that an old white lady was in the back seat,

a serenely sleeping face beneath a cap of curly white hair. Next to her the remaining space in the back had been packed with small suitcases, plastic carrier bags, a worn stuffed donkey, a pile of paperback books and a set of cream coloured padded photograph albums spilling out of a brown paper bag - what looked to me like the random leftovers you get when you move house.

They introduced themselves as the Phillips brothers, the eldest was Richard and the youngest Jasper—they were relocating their mother from her ancestral council flat off Cable Street to a recently constructed Granny flat at chez Phillip in Swindon.

'Only the engine started cutting out,' said Richard.

'We had to push it up from the slip road,' said Jasper.

The AA had been summoned but had yet to arrive.

I asked Jasper to get back in and try to start it again. Through the windscreen I saw his arm tense as he turned the key but absolutely nothing happened.

'It's the electrics, isn't it?' I said.

Richard nodded

'What else could it be?' he asked.

I put my hand on the engine and, much to my surprise, found out.

Magic leaves a trace behind on the material world, we call this trace vestigia. You probably sense it a dozen times a day but until someone teaches you to recognise it then you've probably mistaken it for a memory, or a daydream or just the random misfiring of your neurones.

There was a flash of singing and the smell of rotting seashore, liquorish and sherbet, wet pavement and the flickering cigarette smell of an old cinema.

Once you know what to look for you start to learn to interpret what you sense. Metal retains vestigia for a long time, but this was hot and fresh and newly laid down. It also wasn't the stuff laid down by everyday life or a mercurial intrusion from faerie—this was the same flavour as the vestigia that permeated the shooting range back at the Folly—this is what the Germans called *magievestigium*, the trace left behind when your actual wizard does a spell.

I quickly stepped back from the bonnet and did a three sixty of the car park but saw nothing.

Richard gave me a startled look but before he could speak I showed him my warrant card.

'Where exactly did the engine stop?' I asked.

'Like I said,' he said. 'On the slip road.'

I wondered whether it was worth the time and effort to dig out the Mercedes' electronics to see whether its chipset had been thaumatologically degraded but decided against it. I knew from bitter experience that any microprocessor sitting that close to a spell strong enough to leave that clear vestigia was going to be completely trashed. Besides there was an easier way to check.

'Have either of your phones stopped working?' I asked

'How did you guess?' asked Richard.

I persuaded Richard to hand his over and shook it next to my ear and heard the unmistakable sound of fine sand hissing through the remaining components.

'Same as the electrics,' I said.

'Was it an EMP pulse?' asked Jasper getting out of the car.

'Possibly something like that,' I said. I do like it when members of the public provide their own cover story— saves ever so much time and effort.

'What's an EMP pulse?' asked Richard.

While Jasper explained, getting most of the technical details wrong I noticed, I looked over at where Beverley was waiting impatiently with not-Nicole by the Asbo and beckoned them over.

'Can you keep an eye on the car for me?' I asked Beverley.

'Who's inside,' she asked.

I explained about how the Phillips brothers were relocating their aged mother and how I just needed to pop back up the slip road to see whether a rogue practitioner had nobbled their car.

'Peter,' said Beverley. 'You do know—'

'I'll be really quick,' I said. 'Honest.'

She gave me a sly smile and told me to take my time.

Chieveley Services is one of those rare service stations

that isn't split either side of the motorway. Instead you come off the M4 where it crosses the A34, spin round a roundabout and shoot off down a slip road marked Donnington, Hotel, Services.

The Phillips brothers had limped just close enough to see the BP and COSTA COFFEE sign before the engine had died completely.

'We didn't think it was safe to just leave it here,' said Richard as we stood in the sodium half-light. There was no rough shoulder or pavement, just a strip of grass with a slight upward bank. Traffic was intermittent but I kept a wary eye out for oncoming traffic—drivers come off the motorway with their reflexes tuned to the wrong channel. They don't expect to see people and so they can run you down before they even register your existence.

Just to be on the safe side I walked all the way up to the works entrance and had a good look behind the sparse bushes that utterly failed to screen the service station from the road. The only thing I sensed was the smell of warm tarmac and old diesel.

'What would an EMP look like?' asked Jasper as we walked back.

'It's invisible,' I said. 'You're certain the trouble started while you were on the motorway?'

'Definitely,' said Richard.

'And you didn't notice a vehicle following you at all?' I asked. 'Off the motorway and onto the slipway.'

'There was nothing behind us,' said Jasper. 'I remember because we were slowing down and I was worried something would hit us from behind.'

Having just recently gone mano a caballo with an invisible unicorn, I wasn't about to rule out an unseen follower but that now seemed less likely than that the problem came from inside their car.

We reached the umpteenth mini roundabout and found a short cut through the bushes into the car park. Ahead I saw that the rear passenger door of the Mercedes was open and Beverley was squatting by the door and talking to the occupant. A couple of metres away not-Nicole was lying on her back on the concrete, arms and legs outstretched like a starfish. She did this whenever she got bored or felt neglected—neither me nor Beverley could figure out why.

'Was your mum awake when this happened?' I asked the brothers as we approached.

'Was she awake?' said Richard. 'She was definitely awake.'

'She doesn't like long car journeys,' said Jasper.

'Was she saying anything?' I asked.

'Like what?' asked Richard.

'Oh, I don't know,' I said. 'Something in a foreign language—Latin maybe?'

'Does cockney count as a foreign language?' asked Jasper.

'She was complaining that she wanted to stop,' said Richard.

And then they stopped, I thought as we reached the car.

Beverley got up and gave me a smug smile. I glanced down at the brothers' mother who was wide awake and staring out of the Mercedes with bright blue eyes. I looked back at Beverley who nodded.

I sighed and turned to the brothers Phillips.

'I'm just going to have a quick word with your mum,' I said. 'What's her name.'

'Edna,' said Jasper. 'I'm not sure…'

'I'll just be a moment,' I said. I pointed to a spot five metres away. 'If you two could just wait over there with my colleague.'

They didn't want to leave me alone with their mother but a combination of police authority and the promise that if they would give me five minutes I could sort everything out including their transport saw them shuffle reluctantly away.

Once they were out of earshot I squatted down by the open car door until my face was level with the old lady's and gave her my best police-I'm-just-here-to-help smile.

'Hello Edna, my name's Peter Grant and I'm with the police,' I said. 'How long have you been able to do magic?'

'Cor,' she said. 'Is that what it is—you know I was wondering.'

'What did you think was happening?' I asked.

'I thought I'd developed ESP,' she said. 'Like that girl in the Stephen King book. Only it would have been a lot more useful when I was young, still, why look a gift horse in the mouth? I always say.'

'So when did it start?' I asked.

'Last year,' she said. 'I knew something was wrong when the TV blew up.'

'Can you make a light?' I asked. A werelight is the first thing you learn when you apprentice and it's the sort of 'party trick' that can get passed down within families.

'No,' said Mrs Phillips sounding intrigued. 'Can you?'

I checked both ways to make sure we weren't being overlooked and conjured a werelight, just a small one and just for a moment. Edna's eyes grew even brighter.

'Are you a wizard then?' she asked.

'Apprentice,' I said.

'Hold on,' she said. 'I thought you was the filth.'

'And that as well.'

'Good,' she said. 'Because I want to report a crime.'

'Is it a serious crime?'

'Is kidnapping serious?'

'Very serious,' I said.

'In that case you'd better nick my sons,' she said. 'They're trying to kidnap me.'

'That's a very serious accusation.'

'What else can you call it when you and your possessions are bundled into a car and driven away against your will,' she said.

'You didn't want to leave London then?' I asked.

'They want to relocate me to Swindon,' she said. 'Swindon, I ask you—why would I want to live in Swindon?'

'What's wrong with Swindon?' I asked because I'm a fair-minded guy.

'Nothing as such,' said Mrs Phillips. 'But it never stops at Swindon, does it? Then it's a nice little house in a small village near Swindon, where there's no buses and nothing but cows and fat lady vicars to keep you company.'

I thought the fat lady vicar was unlikely.

'But that's not the worse part,' said the old lady.

'No.'

'After that you find yourself in Wales,' she said.

'No.'

'I've heard them discussing it when they think I'm not listening,' she said. 'Quiet, they say, peaceful, they say. When have I ever wanted peace and quiet? If I hadn't had them both at home I'd reckon there'd been a mix up at the hospital and they'd given me the wrong boys.' She shifted in her seat.

'I mean I have nothing against the Welsh,' she said. 'But their qualities as a nation don't enter into it. I didn't want to leave and they made me and that's kidnapping.'

I glanced over to where the Phillips brothers were staring back at us—probably wondering what the hell was going on—and wished she'd just turned out to be an ethically challenged magician or a ghost or something simple.

I took out my notebook because I had a sudden sinking feeling that I might need an official record of events.

'Why don't you just tell me what happened?'

So she did and the crucial thing, to my mind, was that she still had her council flat and home care visits in place when they took her away. She hadn't wanted to leave and I wasn't at all sure that 'we thought she'd like it better in Swindon', constituted a lawful excuse under the law.

Still before bothering the Thames Valley Police, I thought it was worth talking to the brothers. Which went about the way I thought it might.

'You can't just take our granny away,' said Jasper. 'She's family.'

'She's also legally competent in her own right,' I said. 'If you try to drive off with her while she's protesting, I'll have to stop you.'

'Wait,' said Jasper. 'Are you accusing us of kidnapping our own mother?'

'That's outrageous,' said Richard. 'A classic abuse of police power.'

'No,' I said. 'Your mother is accusing you of kidnapping and I'm exercising a classic bit of police discretion by not arresting you right now and letting the courts sort it out.'

It's amazing how long, sometimes, it takes people to realise they're actually breaking the law. The two brothers stared at me and then turned, as one, to look at their mum who gave them a little wave.

'Fine,' said Richard. 'Arrest us.'

'I don't want to arrest anyone,' I said.

'It's typical of modern Britain,' said Richard. 'You try to do the right thing…'

I let him go on for a while because the alternative usually ends in an arrest and I was desperate to avoid that. Once he'd wound down I explained that they were going to have to return their dear old mum to her former residence.

'If she doesn't want to go,' I said. 'You're not allowed to force her.'

'I get it,' said Jasper. 'Human rights directive and all that but she's not capable of looking after herself.'

'We'll look after her,' said Beverley suddenly.

'I beg your pardon,' said Richard.

And Beverley talked them into it. She didn't even use the influence, out of deference to me I hope, but she spun some serious bullshit about sheltered accommodation and twenty-four-hour nursing quality care. She basically kept on talking until Richard and Jasper gave in. When she'd finished re-ordering their lives,

I drew her back to the Mercedes for a word in her shell-like.

'You can't just be giving old ladies a home,' I said.

'Why not?'

'Because there's thousands of just as perfectly deserving older people who could use your help?' I said.

'Where?' she asked.

'Out there,' I said and waved vaguely in the direction of the east bound carriageway.

'Yeah but this one is right here,' she said. 'And listening to every word we say.'

'Don't mind me, dears,' said Mrs Phillips.

'She's going to live at your mum's house?' I asked. 'What's she going to do all day?'

'Whatever she likes,' said Beverley. 'It's full of my mum's cronies, half of whom are qualified nurses I might add.'

'What about her sons?'

'They can come visit,' she said. 'It's only Wapping.'

'Wapping?' asked Mrs Phillips. 'I used to go drinking at the Prospect of Whitby.'

'That's right next door to my mum's,' Beverley told her and then grinned at me. 'That's practically destiny, that is.'

'Bev,' I said. 'You just can't adopt a granny on a whim.'

'Why not?'

'What about all the other grannies who need help?'

'What about all the other crimes out there that need solving?'

'It's not a long-term solution,' I said.

'She doesn't need a long-term solution,' said Beverley in a quiet voice that made me think before I opened my gob again.

'What do you mean?'

'She's not going to make it to Christmas,' said Beverley. 'Are you, dear?

'Dead by November,' said Mrs Phillips cheerfully. 'I've got brain cancer.'

'Brain cancer?'

'Totally inoperable,' said Mrs Phillips tapping the side of her head with a finger.

'When did you get your ESP?' I asked.

'About a year ago,' said Mrs Phillips.

'And when were you diagnosed?'

'About the same time.'

'Do you think they're related?' Beverley asked me.

'Of course they're related,' said Mrs Phillips. 'It's not likely to be a bleeding coincidence, is it?'

It's an iron rule of mine that I never argue correlation versus causation in the middle of the night, especially when I had an alternative option.

'We're going to take you to see a doctor friend of mine,' I said.

'Not another doctor,' said Edna.

'You'll like this one, he's Scottish,' I said. 'He's going to stick your head in an MRI and then off to Wapping.' And I was just about to add—for a lifetime's supply of deep-fried plantain—when I realised that it wasn't going to be much of a lifetime and stopped myself.

Or maybe I said something out loud because Mrs Phillip cackled and said—'Better than the alternative.' Although in fairness she could have been talking about Swindon.

It took until dawn to rustle up replacement transport for the Phillips brothers, a van to carry Mrs Edna Phillips' belongings back to London. Not-Nicole remained were she was, spread-eagled on the concrete, and apparently slept through the whole thing. Certainly, she seemed surprised when she climbed into the back of the Asbo and found herself sharing with Mrs Phillips.

'Who are you?' she asked.

'I'm the future, kid,' said Mrs Phillips. 'You'd better put your seat belt on because it only gets rougher from here.'

King of The Rats

(*Set between* Foxglove Summer *and* The Hanging Tree)

Introduction

Mail Rail, the Postal Museum's Underground Railway, were announcing their plans to renovate the facility as a historical attraction and asked me whether I could write a short story for the occasion. The result was 'King of the Rats,' ably performed by Ben Bailey Smith (otherwise known as Doc Brown) in the secret train maintenance yard deep under Mount Pleasant sorting office.

Just to clear up any confusion—Melvin is the other occupant of the canoe in *False Value*.

'This is discrimination,' said Melvin.

'No it isn't,' I said—although technically speaking I suspected it was.

'It's because I'm a rat,' he said. 'Isn't it?'

'You're not really a rat,' I said.

'I'm a rat and this is a violation of the human rights act.'

I really wish members of the public would bother to read that bloody act before quoting from it.

'No it isn't,' I said. 'Apart from anything else, if you really are a rat, then the Human Rights Act doesn't apply.'

'Typical,' said Melvin.

I suppose he did look a bit rat-like, being a small white guy with a scraggly beard, and big yellowy front teeth, which he persistently displayed by exaggerating his overbite. Personally, had a simile been required, I would have gone with ferrety. But that would have been to ignore the rat costume he was wearing. It was like an adult-sized pyjama suit, complete with a hood and fake ears. It looked like it had originally been made of felt but had since been covered in so many layers of shit that it was impossible to tell for sure. Literally shit—judging from the smell.

Melvin's head twitched from side to side looking for a way out, but it was in vain—me and Kumar had him well and truly stitched up. Backed into what had once been a storage room of the main maintenance depot of the old Mail Rail.

Back in the good old days of 1911 when London's streets were covered in horse manure and traffic congestion could give you a parasitic infection as well as a headache, the Post Office decided to utilise two new cutting edge technologies—electric rail and the Greathead Shield Tunnel Boring System—to create a mini railway for the post. It would run from Whitechapel to Paddington and allow the mail to glide from one side of the city to the other, untroubled by traffic jams, inclement weather or, during the occasional world war, high explosives. It opened in 1924 and was only closed in 2003 because 'being awesome' no longer registered on the Royal Mail's balance sheet.

Even narrow gauge trains weigh several tons and, unlike its big brother, the Mail Rail didn't conveniently surface in the suburbs to allow maintenance under an open sky. So under Mount Pleasant sorting office an engineering depot was decreed, a great long artificial cavern currently filled with enough spiky cast iron, Bakelite and rheostat-using technology to cause the most jaded industrial archaeologist to swoon.

Running just beside the Engineering Depot is the River Fleet. So when the current owners, the British Postal Museum and Archive, decided that it would make a wonderful corporate entertaining spot, stroke heritage train ride, Fleet naturally took an interest. And where Fleet takes an interest her sister Lady Ty is rarely far behind. It's a Hampstead watershed thing. Which is why when the first planned event—a sort of proof of concept soiree with an obscure literary bent—was gate-crashed by a man in a rat suit, I got called in. Me being the Met's current expert on high maintenance river deities.

I'd dragged in Jaget because ever since we'd invented the triple sewer luge with a visiting FBI agent he'd been my go-to guy for all matters concerning the Underground.

'Is this going to take long?' called Fleet from behind us. She and her sister had found Melvin skulking in a half-flooded maintenance pit just to the left of where they were going to serve canapés.

It's a police rule of thumb that anything involving members of the public takes twice as long as you think it will, so I told Fleet to give us some room to work. No custody sergeant in the city would be happy with me dumping someone this smelly in their nice clean custody suite—not until I'd at least made an effort to palm them off on the mental health system. Plus he didn't look all that compos mentis to me, what with the sniffing and twitching.

'How long have you been a rat?' I asked.

Melvin twitched and rubbed his hand across his cheek.

'About a month,' he said.

'And before that?' I asked.

'Before that what?'

'Well you told us your name was Melvin,' I said. 'What's your surname?'

'Norvegicus,' he said.

'Rattus norvegicus,' said Jaget. 'Latin for rat.' And, it turned out, an LP by a band called The Stranglers— although Jaget admitted that he didn't think that last fact was relevant.

'Did you have a different name before you were a rat?' I asked, proving once more that politely asking the same bleeding question again and again is the backbone of modern policing.

'Starkey—my name was Starkey.'

'Melvin Starkey?'

Melvin nodded and Jaget wrote it down.

'What do you do for a living Melvin?' asked Jaget.

'I scurry,' said Melvin. 'And hurry and fight the dogs and kill the cats.'

Jaget made another note—obviously thinking that we should check with Islington Environmental Health and the RSPCA.

'What about before you were a rat?' asked Jaget.

'I was an estate agent,' he said.

'And where did you live?'

He gave us an address in Primrose Hill.

Me and Jaget stepped back so we could talk amongst ourselves. Melvin stayed where he was, squatting on his haunches, nose twitching and his pathetic felt ears bobbing back and forth.

'I think we have enough for an ID,' I said.

'Can you handle him on your own?' asked Jaget.

I said I could and he trotted off to find a place where his airwave would work.

Fleet and Lady Ty glided forward, champagne glasses in their hands and a determined look in their eyes.

'So is it to be a prisoner transport?' asked Fleet. 'Or an ambulance?'

'Or pest control?' said Lady Ty. 'I'm sure Fleet would be happy to whoosh him down to the Thames if you wanted a discreet disposal.'

'Really?' I said. 'Is that something you've done before?'

Fleet smiled at her sister. 'He's so suspicious these days.'

'We're just offering.' said Lady Ty. 'I'm sure you have better things to do.'

'You called me. Remember?'

'Fair point,' said Fleet. 'Do you think he's under the influence?'

He was under the influence, alright. I just couldn't tell what of: drugs, alcohol, misfiring brain cells—magic?

'Why don't you stand back and let me work,' I said.

Lady Ty looked at Fleet and they both giggled. I hoped that it was the alcohol because I didn't like the idea of the Goddess of the River Tyburn giggling—it was disturbing on so many levels.

I went back to Melvin the Rat and tried to narrow down the possibilities.

'So when did you decide to become a rat?' I asked.

'It's not a question of wanting to be a rat,' said Melvin. 'It just sort of happens to you. All of a sudden you realise that's what you want to be.'

'And this realisation came a month ago?'

'Yeah,' said Melvin. 'Have you got any cheese?'

'My colleague has gone to fetch some,' I said. 'Can you remember what you were doing?'

'I was asking about a house,' he said.

Specifically: making inquiries into whether a particular person might want to sell their four storey Georgian terrace on St. Mark's Crescent near Regent's Park. Melvin thought it was worth a go because the same person had owned the house since 1956 and in that period the value had risen from merely expensive to ludicrous.

'I was hoping it would be an old lady,' said Melvin who explained that he was particularly skilled at talking the old dears into relinquishing their property. 'I play fair, though,' he said. 'I make sure they get a good price.'

Presumably the 'old dears' then headed for Hastings or Bournemouth with a nice capital nest egg and the streets of Camden were made safe for the super-rich.

'So did you persuade her to sell?'

'I don't remember,' said Melvin. 'And in any case, that's when I realised my true nature.'

'Do you remember going up to the front door?'

'Yes,' he said. 'I remember that.'

'Did you ring the doorbell?'

'Yes,' said Melvin and explained that he remembered the door opening and there being a smell, a strong animal smell, like something from a zoo.

And then his true nature as a rat became clear and off he scampered towards his office on Camden Parkway.

He couldn't remember anything about the woman who answered the door.

He'd acquired the rat suit at Escapade's costume shop in Chalk Farm and had naturally found himself drawn to the sewers. I asked him how he ended up underneath Mount Pleasant and he said it was an accident—he'd been searching for a bite of cheese and had just followed his nose.

'This is your lucky day,' I said. 'Not only am I going to introduce you to a nice Scottish doctor, so you can be checked out, you're going to be provided with cheese and old rope and whatever else it is your little ratty heart desires.'

And you'll stick your head in an MRI, give blood samples and throw the gauntlet of science into the face of the inexplicable. Although I expected Dr Walid might want to get him washed up first. The key thing being that it wouldn't be me trying to get him into a shower.

So when Jaget got back we arranged for Dr Walid to come and take Melvin to a place of safety under Section 136 of the Mental Health Act. Jaget had confirmed Melvin's identity and that he had been reported missing a month earlier. Once we had him wrapped in a blanket and stuffed into the back of an ambulance I popped back inside.

I asked Fleet and Lady Ty whether they knew anything about the address on St Mark's Crescent.

'No, nothing,' said Lady Ty.

'I never go down that way,' said Fleet. 'I'm not really a Primrose Hill, Regent's Park person. When I want to go for a walk, I go up the heath. Although the view from the top of the hill is really good.'

Which just goes to show that Lady Ty is a much better liar than Fleet.

Still I knew better than to try the direct approach with these two. So off I went, with my constabulary duty still to be done.

* * *

St Mark's Crescent was Georgian semis down one side and a slightly later terrace on the other. According to Google Earth the semis all backed onto the Grand Union Canal which would have been enough to raise my suspicions even if Jaget's IIP check hadn't thrown up that the ground rent, mortgage, rates and then council tax had all been paid by London Zoo since the early 1960s.

So we swapped my Asbo for Jaget's even more inconspicuous Vauxhall Corsa and staked out the house. We were just getting bored enough to consider playing 'how much do you reckon that house is worth?'—a favourite game amongst Londoners—when a Forest Green Range Rover pulled up outside and Lady Ty and Fleet disembarked.

We let them get halfway up the front steps before making ourselves known in the time honoured police manner.

'Oi!' I called. 'What do you think you're doing?'

'Oh shit,' said Fleet.

'Told you,' said Lady Ty.

'We just want to have a quiet word,' said Fleet. 'No need for this to get all official.'

'A quite word with who?' I asked.

'Whom,' said Jaget.

'With whom?' I asked, taking Jaget's word for it.

'We think she's the spirit of the Grand Union Canal,' said Fleet.

'Like you are with the rivers?'

'No,' said Lady Ty firmly, 'not like us.'

'Definitely not,' said Fleet. 'Canals are tricky and, anyway, she may also have something to do with London Zoo.'

'Oh really,' said Jaget obviously remembering who was paying the council tax. 'What makes you think that?'

'She's an orang-utan,' said Fleet.

On that we all withdrew to a safe distance while Fleet and Lady Ty explained.

'We think she was brought over to be a mate of Charlie—the first orang-utan to be kept in the monkey house. But she escaped before she could be settled in.' The Grand Union Canal actually bisects the zoo and it was feared that she'd gone into it. Word of the escape was kept secret and, this being the 1950s, the secret was kept.

'We only found out about her when we went for a walk down the tow path,' said Fleet. 'We were minding our own business when this ape woman came out of nowhere and started haranguing us.'

Apparently she had some kind of aggro with Mama Thames, but the sisters had never found out how it started.

'You don't ask Mum about that kind of stuff,' said Fleet. 'Not unless you want to be on suicide duty for a year straight.'

'But this is the last straw,' said Lady Ty. 'Unless you believe it was a coincidence that Melvin the Rat turned up at a party we were hosting.'

Actually I thought it probably was, but I found that when people are nursing a grievance it's a waste of time trying to explain the ubiquitous nature of coincidence in the universe. People always want things to happen for a reason.

'So, to recap,' said Jaget. 'A female orang-utan who may be the goddess…'

'Spirit,' said Lady Ty and Fleet together.

'…who may be the spirit of the Great Western Canal and/or London, is the most likely suspect to have convinced Melvin that he is a rat?'

'Pretty much,' I said. 'Let's go and have a word with her.'

'You should leave this to us,' called Fleet after us as we headed towards the house. 'She'll have you for breakfast.'

'Tell you what,' I called back as Jaget rang the bell. 'If we're not out in half an hour, you can come and rescue us.'

A Rare Book of Cunning Device

(Set between The Hanging Tree *and* Lies Sleeping)

Introduction

I am a great believer in libraries and so I jumped at a chance to do an exclusive audio story for Audible with the proceeds going to a library charity. Obviously the story had to be about a library and what better library to choose than the British Library with its five underground levels full of rare books.

'Aha,' said the Librarian. 'You must be Mamusu's boy.'

The Librarian was a tiny round faced white woman who appeared to be dressed in several layers of brightly-coloured cardigans.

I confirmed that I was that Peter Grant and she beamed at me.

'I knew your mum back in Freetown when she was just a wee slip of a girl,' she said.

'Did you?' I asked stupidly, because I was having trouble code-shifting from job to family acquaintance. Especially one who used my mum's Sierra Leonean name. Most white people that know her call her Rose— even my dad.

'I came to your christening,' she said. 'Enormous party, food was brilliant.'

'I'll tell her we met,' I said.

'I wonder if she'll remember me,' she said.

'What's your name?' I asked.

'I haven't said, have I?'

'No.'

'Ah, yes,' she held out a hand for me to shake. 'Elsie Winstanley. I'm the Specialist Collection Manager. Thank you for coming.'

'My pleasure,' I said. 'What seems to be the problem?'

'We appear to have acquired a poltergeist,' she said.

This seemed unlikely.

According to the massed wisdom of the practitioners who came before me—which was corroborated, at least in part, by my own research—ghosts, poltergeists and other incorporeal phenomena fed off the vestigia that accumulates in the fabric of the material world. This build-up takes time and while stone, brick and even concrete retain vestigia well, a building generally had to be at least thirty years old before acquiring any ghosts. More than a hundred years for a poltergeist or something more exotic.

The British Library had been built in 1997 and was less then seventeen years old.

It was an odd building, too. A sort of collision between the monumental brick-built bulk of a 1930s power station and the strange post-modernist desire to recreate that famous Escher interior. You know, the one with all the perspective-defying staircases.

Ms Winstanley had met me in the foyer where I was issued with a security pass, because not even a warrant card gets you backstage at the second largest book collection in the world.

Behind the reception desk rose the King's Library—a six storey glass tower containing 65,000 books donated by King George III during a rare fit of sanity. There are theories that he feared, in his madness, that they were possessed of unquiet spirits and felt he could not sleep soundly under the same roof. Or, more likely to my mind, he felt the palace needed the shelf space. Still, that was a lot of historical material. So I wasn't about to dismiss the claim out of hand.

'What makes you think you've got a poltergeist?' I asked.

'Things have been moved around during the night,' she said. 'Doors that should be closed have been left open and some books have been found on the wrong shelf.'

'You're sure it isn't just…'

'Yes, we're sure,' she said. 'We're librarians. We notice this sort of thing. And in any case while books may, occasionally, mislay themselves, priceless sixteenth century globes do not.'

'It was stolen?'

'It was moved from one end of the basement to the other,' she said.

'Well, perhaps somebody needed the space,' I said.

'This—,' began Ms Winstanley, and then changed her

mind. 'I think it will be easier just to show you the basement.'

Which she did—all four sodding floors. All with very tight security, particularly the top-secret sections where they keep the classified maps from the Ministry of Defence.

'Things don't move about of their own accord,' said Ms Winstanley. 'Not in this library.'

So I did a preliminary IVA, or Initial Vestigia Assessment, and because it was a sodding big building with four floors of basements it took me most of the afternoon.

'It mostly manifests itself at night,' said Ms Winstanley when we stopped for coffee.

It certainly wasn't manifesting itself to me.

I noted down all the details, thanked Ms Winstanley for the tour and headed back to the Folly. There I planned to fill in one of our brand spanking new Falcon Incident Report forms and file it, until Nightingale came back from hunting big cats in Norfolk.

Only I got back to find our archivist, Professor Harold Postmartin, DPhil, FRS, enjoying tea in the atrium. I made the mistake of telling him about the alleged poltergeist in the library, because he might find it of interest, and his face lit up. I know that look of enthusiasm and the last time I saw it I ended up covered in pesticide and wrestling with a tree.

'Not "Hatbox" Winstanley?' said Postmartin.

I described her as best as I could, and Postmartin confirmed that it was the woman he was thinking of. So called because she was said to have travelled down the Amazon in a hatbox, swam the English Channel wearing nothing but goose fat and ran a library in Kolwezi until she was forcibly evacuated by the French Foreign Legion.

'I'm almost certain that the last two are true,' said Postmartin. 'And if old Hatbox says there's something supernatural in her stacks, then I for one would take her very seriously indeed.'

So back we both went to the British Library, where Ms Winstanley, upon hearing that Postmartin was staying the night, insisted that she join us in our ghost hunting exploits.

'Not only am I intensely curious to see what you boys actually get up to,' she said, 'but also you cannot leave these university types unsupervised amongst your stacks. They're famously light fingered and they don't call Harold "Postmartin the Pirate" for nothing.'

When I asked who called Postmartin a pirate, and why, she merely winked and said that while she'd love to tell me it was still subject to the Thirty Year Rule.

'Official Secrets Act and all that,' she said.

As revenge I popped back and fetched Toby. When Ms Winstanley objected, I told her that Toby was a highly trained police dog.

She gave Toby a sceptical look.

'Trained in what?' she asked.

'Many strange things,' I said. 'Of which the uninitiated is not meant to know.'

'Are,' said Ms Winstanley. '"Are not meant to know", not "is".'

And that is why I don't normally argue with librarians.

So me and one of the security staff carried gear down to the basement while Ms Winstanley and Postmartin compared Ninja Librarian notes.

We were making camp in one of the central workrooms on Basement 2. Underground, the workspaces and stacks were as generously proportioned as a billionaire's basement, with high ceilings and wide corridors. Everything that wasn't painted 1970s sci-fi white was a brilliant red or blue, causing me to have an almost irresistible urge to tattoo my eyeball and parkour my way up the walls.

The ceilings had to be high, because not only did the bookshelves go up over two metres but above them ran the Paternoster book delivery system. Essentially the same as the baggage handling system in a major airport, only designed not to destroy the packages they were carrying. Ms Winstanley had explained how it worked on the first tour. Readers, upstairs in one of the many reading rooms, order a book on the computer, the book gets pulled off one of the 625 kilometres of shelf, put in a box, the box goes on the patented Paternoster book delivery system and is carried upstairs where... you can guess the rest.

By law the British Library gets two copies of every book published in the UK and Ireland. Which adds up to a lot of books—over fourteen million so far.

'Although the vast majority of the Mills and Boons collection is kept at Boston Spa,' said Ms Winstanley.

And that wasn't counting the 260 thousand journals, four million maps and sixty million patents.

'Sixty million?'

'Oh, yes,' said Ms Winstanley. 'People are extraordinarily inventive.'

'Obviously,' I said.

'Most of them are complete tosh of course,' she said.

There were specialist bookcases for old, rare and strangely shaped books, but most of the stock was kept in huge ranks of mechanical bookcases, the kind that close together to minimise floor space. When you wanted a book you found the right section and turned a handle which drove a series of gears that prised two of the shelves apart to form a temporary aisle. The gearing was high and the shelves were heavy. Ms Winstanley must have spotted me testing the weight with my shoulder.

'Oh, you have to make sure people know you're in there,' she said. 'Otherwise somebody might close it and you'd be squished.'

'Whoever knew this job was so dangerous?' I said

'Ah, yes, librarianship,' said Ms Winstanley. 'It's not for the faint hearted.'

By eleven o'clock that evening we were all set up, so we cracked open one of the industrial sized thermoses I'd brought from the Folly while we waited for the last of the staff to vacate the basement. Even the security staff were leaving, so we wouldn't mistake them for a marauding poltergeist.

Since neither our phones or my airwave or my, now patent pending, magic detectors would work in the basement our strategy was to leave at least one person at the base camp while the others went out as a single group and didn't split up under any circumstances. Team Folly was not at home for Mr Scooby Doo.

'Particularly since I am, in fact, the only one of us who knows their way around,' said Ms Winstanley.

So a little bit before twelve me, Toby and Ms Winstanley went for our first patrol leaving Postmartin to hold the fort.

What with the sloppy procedure, the size of the basement, the lack of any detection equipment and the newness of the building, I thought it was pretty unlikely that we were going to discover anything during this or any subsequent night's searching.

So of course, less than half an hour later, we practically tripped over the bloody thing.

There's a particular kind of spookiness about being brightly lit and underground. The constant fluorescent light pushes at your peripheral vision and the absence of shadows flattens out your perspective. It also doesn't help that the climate control system is prone to random ticks and hums.

We started with the closest of the caged-in areas set aside for holding rare, valuable or classified parts of the collection.

'Or more likely because these are the last empty shelves available,' said Ms Winstanley as she unlocked the gate and let us into the first one. The stacks inside had large shelves holding big leather-bound books that looked like props for a fantasy film. The tan and brown of the covers were brilliant against the sterile grey-white of the shelves. I wanted to reach out and run my fingers along their spines to see if some of the history would rub off—but I'm better trained than that.

I caught Toby eyeing up the corner of the stack, so I tugged on his lead to make him behave.

'This is mainly—' started Ms Winstanley, but before she could finish her sentence something shot past our feet and scuttled out the open gate. I didn't get much beyond the impression that it was bigger than Toby, angular, brown and had lots of legs.

By the time I'd activated enough neurons to run to the cage door, the thing had gone.

'Tell me that wasn't a spider?' said Ms Winstanley in a deceptively calm tone.

'Can't have been,' I said.

'Thank god for that,' she said. 'Can't stand spiders.'

'It was too big,' I said. 'You can't scale an exoskeleton up that far.' The inverse square law can be such a comfort sometimes. Plus I definitely remembered something about gas diffusion and box lungs or something like that.

'So magic can't make things bigger?' asked Ms Winstanley, and I really wished she hadn't.

'It definitely wasn't a poltergeist,' I said. 'That much is certain.'

I looked at Toby who hadn't reacted until the thing, whatever it was, ran past him. And I hadn't registered a hint of vestigia either. Perhaps it wasn't magical at all—could it be mechanical, electronic—a machine? The spider configuration was considered a good shape for autonomous robots.

'I brought the wrong gear,' I said.

We should have had cameras, motion detectors and infrared sensors—isn't that always the way? You set out to hunt a ghost and you trip over a robot instead.

'Shouldn't we go after it?' asked Ms Winstanley.

'Let's see if we can't find out what it was doing in here,' I said.

I found marks on the sides of the stacks, and more

on one of the posts that supported the wire metal cage on the opposite side. The shelves were full of exactly the books Ms Winstanley said she expected to be there, some hugely valuable, some historically significant.

'All of them priceless,' she said.

'Anything missing?'

Ms Winstanley said she couldn't tell without checking the catalogue on a terminal back at base camp. So we trooped back and I briefed Postmartin and suggested that we call it a night.

'Nonsense,' said Postmartin. 'Where's your sense of adventure?'

I said it was back at the Folly with my forensic collection kit, motion sensors and Taser. He literally said 'pish', which I'd never heard a real person say in my life.

'We should at least give deduction a chance,' he said. 'Is it possible it was a book?'

'It had legs,' I said.

'There's a long history of extraordinary things being hidden in books,' said Postmartin. 'Alcohol, keys, letters, very small heirs to a throne…'

'Hand grenades,' said Ms Winstanley without looking up from her terminal.

'When was that?' asked Postmartin.

'Bulawayo,' she said. 'In '75.'

'Hand grenades, pistols, radios,' said Postmartin. 'Why not a robot?'

A book robot seemed a bit Despicable Me to me, but why not?

Once Ms Winstanley had her list it took us less than five minutes to locate the space on the shelves, above head height of course, where a book was missing.

'A Book of Cunning Device,' said Ms Winstanley, reading the details off her tablet. 'Attributed to Salman ibn Jabir al Rasheed, a tenth century scholar from Bagdad.'

'Why attributed?' I asked.

There was a theory, explained Ms Winstanley, that the book didn't originate in the Islamic Near East at all, that it had been manufactured in the West, probably Venice, in imitation of the works that were being brought home from the Holy Land by pilgrims and crusaders.

'Like a cargo cult object,' she said. 'Because if you look at the so called 'writing', and you have any Arabic or Farsi at all, it's clear that it's nothing like real Arabic. Not even close.'

She showed me pictures—lines of squiggly text running across a page. The images were poor and, judging by the colour saturation, derived from mid-twentieth century photography. But it looked to me like the writing had been done in gold ink.

'Last catalogued in 1972,' said Ms Winstanley. 'And poorly done at that. We were waiting for our Persian specialist to get back from holiday and have a look.'

Another image showed what looked like a musical

instrument built into the body of the book. Like a horizontal harp with pegs to adjust tension—a horizontal dulcimer, what they called a santur in Iran and Iraq. I recognised it from an album my dad had by the bloke from Deep Forest.

'Or perhaps a musical instrument disguised as a book,' said Ms Winstanley. 'Intriguing, no?'

I asked why, if it was so intriguing, it hadn't been catalogued yet which caused Ms Winstanley to snort.

'There's never enough people to get through your backlog,' said Postmartin. 'That's the curse of librarianship. If your library is of any quality at all, then its collection is going to outpace your manpower.'

I spotted Toby sniffing around another corner of the stacks and moved smartly to stop him marking his territory. But I saw he was sniffing at something at his head height. It looked like the sort of scuff mark left behind by the foot of a tripod or the stud of a football boot.

There was a second further up the stack and a third and a fourth making a trail to an empty shelf far enough up for me to need to use a kick stool to reach it.

'And that's where the book was kept,' said Ms Winstanley.

I put my gloves on, just in case, and reached gingerly into the empty shelf.

And there it was; a vibration like the wind breathing through the strings of a harp and a cascade of notes like running water. It was magical, then, which was a bit of a relief, given that the alternative was super-science—and I really didn't want to have to explain that to Nightingale.

'That globe that was moved,' I said. 'Where exactly did you find it?'

* * *

The uppermost basement was much larger than the ones below and most of the space was taken up with the kind of heavy engineering required to keep 165 kilometres of shelving at just the right temperature and humidity. Plus the humans using the building above, of course, but that was pretty much an afterthought. Unlike the book storage areas below, which had been mainly grey and white with red trimming, the plant rooms were silver with huge cylinders painted blue, connected with yellow pipes.

Definitely the boss level, I thought as we crept through it.

Both Ms Winstanley and Postmartin followed me in because neither wanted to be left behind. Ms Winstanley was carrying Toby because he most definitely had wanted to be left behind. But fortunately I had a stash of Molly's home cooked sausages on hand to bribe him with.

The misplaced globe had been found close to the central air conditioning unit that served the six-storey tower which housed the King's Collection. The unit itself was a huge blue metal box capped with silver and vanishing upwards into a web of silver struts and pipes at roof level. A row of chunky green boxes, like the lockers at a gym, festooned with yellow and black warning markers housed the power regulators.

'I don't want to cramp your style,' shouted Postmartin over the roar of the air conditioners, 'but I'd be rather careful about using magic just here. A moment of over-enthusiasm and it's goodbye priceless national treasure.'

'Great,' I said. 'I'll just ask it to come quietly then.'

'Might be worth a try,' he said.

Toby growled softly and belched.

I followed his gaze and saw movement just behind a pillar of silver metal pipes and bracing struts. Judging by the yellow and black hazard flashes, tampering with them could result in electrocution, suffocation and/or freezing.

Or, more seriously, should I allow books to be damaged, death by librarian.

I told the librarians to stay where they were and advanced—cautiously.

I stopped when I had a good view. It was hanging off a junction box by, I estimated, eight of its ten legs. These I saw were cables made from thinner strands twisted together—perhaps a deployment of the dulcimer strings.

The book part was open like a pair of wings or a carapace and hid how the cables connected to the main body. It was trembling as it clutched the junction box and occasionally a twitch would ripple along the gripping legs. I had the strange impression that it was feeding, but off what? Electricity? That would be pretty bloody unprecedented, magically speaking, not to mention astonishing in something crafted in 9th-century Bagdad.

But obviously not impossible.

It had been the leathery book cover that had put me in mind of a huge insect. But now that it was staying still, I found it a lot less frightening. Right up to the point where it leaped off the box and went for my face.

I don't like insects—never have.

I jumped backwards so hard that I practically landed on my bum and looked up just in time to see the Cunning Device skittering over the concrete floor towards me.

I ran. And I'm still impressed with the way I managed to flip over and get my legs under me before the bloody thing reached me. I went haring down a corridor of silver pipes and blue tanks towards a chunky looking fire door. I didn't dare risk looking behind me and I doubted I'd hear the pitter-patter of legs over the industrial noise of the air conditioning.

Do you know that moment in a film when someone on foot is being chased by a car and, instead of veering onto the pavement and hiding in a doorway or behind a bollard, they keep running straight ahead until they get run down?

I like to learn from the mistakes of fictional characters, so at the next opportunity I veered left down a corridor formed by rows of storage lockers. There, freed from the risk of committing treasonable levels of property damage, I turned, took a deep breath and prepared an impello. I figured my best bet was to flip it on its back and then pin it down.

I stood ready, keeping my mind clear and waiting.

And waiting.

Now, the thing is, you need a clear mind to do magic properly. And the thing about a clear mind is that it allows you to think rationally about your actions. So when the Cunning Device walked past my position—quite slowly I noticed—and blithely continued on its way, I was slightly insulted to be honest.

So I stepped out after it had gone past to see what it did next.

Which turned out to be, bang into the door. It stepped back and tried again—harder this time but the door was designed as a serious fire break and was too heavy. The Cunning Device skipped half a metre to the left and banged against the wall on that side and then repeated the manoeuvre a metre to the right. Then it rotated slowly in place as if having a good look round before returning up the corridor towards me.

Now that it wasn't chasing me I could see that the Cunning Device didn't move that fast. The tips of its long spindly legs skittered on the smooth concrete floors. What it needed, I decided, was a set of tiny slippers or, more practically, friction pads on the ends of its legs.

I considered jumping on it and snapping its covers shut—the way you're supposed to with an alligator's jaws—but I was getting a handle on its behaviour, so I stepped smartly out of its way and followed behind.

Salman ibn Jabir al Rasheed, I thought, you must have been well chuffed with yourself when you built this. And we may only know you through your work, but what a piece of work it is.

'What can you tell me about this Salman al Rasheed?' I asked Ms Winstanley when she and Postmartin joined the parade.

Almost nothing, as it turned out. He was mentioned in a text from 10th-century Bagdad as having been a worthy successor to the Banū Mūsā, the famous trio of inventive brothers, and as the author of The Book of Cunning Device—and that was it.

'It's not that unusual,' said Postmartin. 'There're many people we only really know from their work.'

'Shakespeare for example,' said Ms Winstanley. 'Came from Stratford, went to London, wrote plays, was a genius, retired back to Stratford with the fruits of his pen. His will, his grave, the house he used to live in is just about all we have. And the plays of course, the glorious plays.'

'You don't think they might have been—'

'No,' said both librarians simultaneously.

'Our Salman is seven hundred years older still,' said Ms Winstanley. 'He could have been the toast of Baghdad in his day, but there's no guarantee we would have heard of him.'

I wondered how close we'd come to having a magic-robot-based industrial revolution in the tenth century, and what had happened to prevent it. I decided that, for the moment, I was going to add that question to the long list of what my cousin Abigail has taken to calling The Big Bumper Fun Book of Unanswered Questions (001.098).

So we trooped after the Cunning Device as best we could, as it worked its way back down to Basement 2, via the Paternoster book delivery system I noticed, and returned itself to its assigned shelf in the book cage.

'What now?' asked Ms Winstanley.

I didn't think it was a good idea to let an unclassified magical device run around inside the nation's rare book collection. So I asked Postmartin whether the Folly, under one of its many agreements, had the authority to confiscate dangerous magical artefacts.

'As a matter of fact, I rather think we do,' said Postmartin.

'Now, see here, Harold,' said Ms Winstanley, but Postmartin held up a placating hand.

'We'll call it a loan and craft a nice tailor-made storage facility,' he said.

Inside a Faraday cage, I thought, inside a room panelled with greenwood and cork boards and other non-magically conductive stuff.

'You can research under controlled conditions and partake of Molly's growing range of afternoon teas,' he said. I think afternoon tea might have clinched it because Ms Winstanley deflated. But only a little.

'I told you he was a pirate, didn't I?' she said.

PART TWO

THE OTHERS' STORIES

Introduction

I suppose it was inevitable that other characters would start to agitate for a piece of the action. After all, everyone is the hero of their own story and doesn't see why they couldn't be the protagonist. So I wrote a couple of very short fictions in the hope of keeping them happy. This was a mistake since it neither appeased Nightingale nor Agent Reynolds, and it also led to the creation of a brand new character—Tobias Winter.

But since the principle had been established it meant I now felt free to use different characters for the short stories—much to Peter's relief since this reduced his operational tempo and gave him some time off.

So prepare to meet a baby river, Germany's answer to magical policing and, of course, one very dedicated follower of fashion.

A Dedicated Follower of Fashion

(Set all the way back in the swinging sixties)

Introduction

The trouble with London, from a writer's point of view, is there is so much of it—extending in all directions including into the past. Every time I visit somewhere in the city I'm always asked when I'm going to include their local river in the books. My answer is always the same, the river goes in when I have a story that includes them and whether or not I have a story depends on whether I can find a satisfying personality that fits the river.

So it was only when I discovered that the Huguenot weavers established their cloth factories along the banks of the River Wandle that I had a sudden insight what kind of Goddess would live in a river like that. So having established that she was the Goddess of Schmutter I wondered where she might have come from.

You know that song by The Kinks? Not that one. The other one. No, not that one either. Yeah, that one—'Dedicated Follower of Fashion'. You wouldn't believe it to look at me now, but that song's about me.

These days my daughter does her best to keep me looking respectable, and I haven't the heart to tell her that I'd much rather wear my nice comfortable corduroy trousers, with braces, and leave my shirt untucked. But back in the sixties I was *the* dedicated follower of fashion. And it's true that they sought me here and they sought me there but, as Ray Davies knew perfectly well, that was probably because of the drug dealing. What can I say? Clothes aren't cheap.

I was a middleman buying wholesale and supplying a network of dealers, mostly in and around the King's Road. I rarely sold retail, although I did have a number of select clients. And of course, nothing lubricates a soirée like a bowl full of alpha-methylphenethylamine.

It was all going swimmingly until some little shit from Islington stiffed me on a payment and I found myself coming up ten grand short. And, believe me, ten grand in 1967 was a lot of money. You could buy a house in Notting Hill for less than that—not that anyone wanted to, not in those days.

Now, I'll admit that as an entrepreneur working in such a volatile industry, I probably should have ensured that I had a cash reserve stashed away against such an eventuality. Mistakes were definitely made. But in my defence, not only had I just discovered the joys of blow, I was also distracted by my infatuation with Lilith.

Now, I've always cheerfully swung both ways and, to be honest, I've always been more attracted by the cut of someone's trousers than what was held therein. But when I met Lilith it was as if all the cash registers rung out in celebration. She was so like a man in some ways and so like a woman in others. I'd love to say that it was the best of both worlds but looking back it was a disaster in every respect. Although a completely exhilarating disaster, like a roller coaster to an unknown destination. I tried explaining what she was like to Ray Davies and that beardy writer who ran that sci-fi magazine, but they both got her completely wrong.

So there I was, suddenly ten grand down to people whose names you're better off not knowing—let's just call them the Deplorables and leave it at that. If I tell you that their nicknames were Cutter, Lead Pipe and Gnasher, that should give you a flavour of their character. You could call Cutter the brains behind the gang but that would be risking an overstatement. Organised crime in the good old days required little in the way of actual brains and relied much more on a calculated defiance of the social niceties vis-à-vis psychotic violence. Terrify your rivals, bully your customers, and hand out a bung to the local constabulary and you were away.

And it goes without saying that aesthetically they were a dead loss.

The Deplorables had a straightforward approach to those that owed them money which I will leave to your imagination—suffice only to say that it involved a sledgehammer and, of all things, a marlinspike.

But I had no intention of losing my knees, so I had arranged a couple of new deals that would net me a sufficient profit to cover both what I owed the Deplorables and the same again to appease them sufficiently to save my poor knees from a fate worse than polyester.

I know some of you are thinking that polyester was hip and groovy back in the Swinging Sixties but trust me when I say that it was an abomination from the start— whatever the elegance of its long-chain polymers.

In order to keep body and wardrobe together while I waited for these deals to come to fruition I decanted, along with Lilith and my faithful sidekick Merton, to a squat in Wandsworth just off the Earlsfield High Street. Now, I normally shun the transpontine reaches of the capital. But my thinking was sound. With my reputation as a flower of Chelsea and the King's Road, I reckoned that nobody—least of all the dim members of the Deplorables—would think to look for me across the river.

'No fucking way,' said Lilith when she first saw it, 'am I living in this shithole.'

Squats come in many flavours. Be it political, religious or student, they are almost always shitholes. However, I could see this one had potential and Nigel, God bless his woollen Woolworths socks, had at least kept it clean.

But not particularly tidy.

Outwardly Nigel was definitely one of the children of Aquarius. Inside he had the soul of an accountant, but alas none of the facility with numbers.

According to Nigel, who could be dull about this sort of thing, the building we were squatting in had been built in the eighteenth century as an inn that specialised in serving the trade along the river. This was news to me, because I had assumed the rank channel immediately behind the house was a canal.

'There used to be factories up and down the river,' he told me despite my best efforts to stop him, 'all connected up with barges. And this is where the watermen used to get their drinks in.'

With the collapse of that trade it was converted into a

grand town house, a status it retained for a hundred years or so before providing slum housing for the unwashed multitude. Occasionally, on its hundred-year odyssey, it would surface into the light of respectable society before descending once more into the depths of squalor.

Which is where yours truly arrived to bring a touch of colour and a modicum of good taste to the old place.

Looking back, I believe that might have been the start of the whole ghastly business.

Now, the thing about the drug trade is that it overlaps with the general smuggling industry. As a result, a man with the right contacts can acquire much in the way of valuable cloth—Egyptian cotton and the like—without troubling the good people of Her Majesty's Customs and Excise. Then such an individual might use his reputation for fashion to sell on said items to the East End rag trade at less than wholesale, cash under the table, no questions asked, and no invoices raised. Not as lucrative as a suitcase full of horse, but safer and more dependable.

Cloth, even expensive cloth, takes up considerably more room even than Mary Jane, so the fact that the old building had a beer cellar capacious enough to store the stock was the other reason I'd chosen it as a bolt-hole. Merton and I pressed Nigel into service to help us carry the bales, wrapped in tarpaulin for protection, down to the cellar, which proved to be mercifully dry and cool.

It was surprisingly cool—you could have used it as a pantry.

'That's because of the river,' Nigel explained. 'It's just the other side of that wall.'

I touched the wall and was surprised to find it cool but bone dry.

'They knew how to build houses in those days,' said Nigel.

Once we'd moved the goods in, it was time to deal with the ever simmering domestic crisis that was life with Lilith. In the latest instalment of the drama, she had ejected Nigel from the master bedroom and claimed it as her own. This was less of a distraction than it might have been because Nigel, like nearly all men, was clearly smitten with Lilith and acquiesced with surprisingly good grace.

And so we settled in companionably enough, especially when Lilith and Nigel discovered a common interest in the works of Jack Kerouac. I could see that at some point I would be bedding down with Merton for a night or two. I won't lie and say that I didn't find Lilith's peccadillos upsetting but Merton, bless his acrylic Y-fronts, offered compensation in his own rough manner.

Things started to go wrong the night of the storm and consequent flood. And while our decision to drop acid and commune with the thunder—Nigel's idea, by the way—probably wasn't to blame, it certainly didn't help.

I don't normally do hallucinogenics as they often disappoint. You go up expecting Yellow Submarine and get a lot of irritating visual distraction instead. My colour sense is quite keen enough, thank you, without having a pair of purple velvet bell-bottoms start to shine like a neon sign.

The master bedroom—now Lilith's domain—contained, of all things, a king-size four-poster bed that was missing its curtains. But, since I'd arrived, it at least had matching cotton sheets in a tasteful orange and green fleurs-de-lis pattern. They matched the old wallpaper with its geometric tan and orange florets that still showed the rectangular ghosts of long vanished photographs and paintings.

At some point—Nigel said the 1930s—the owners had installed an aluminium-framed picture window that ran almost the length of the room and looked out over the canal, or more importantly, up into the boiling clouds of the oncoming storm.

Lilith started on the bed with all three of us, but I can't take anything seriously when heading up on LSD, least of all sex. So I quickly disengaged and chose to sit on the end of the bed and watch the storm. I doubt the others were troubled by my absence.

I watched the storm come in over the rooftops of South London with lightning flashing in my eyes and that glorious sense of joy that only comes from something psychoactive interacting with your neurones. I lost myself in that storm and, in it, I thought I sensed the roar of the god of joy, whose acolytes dance naked on the hilltops and rip the goats apart.

But the mind is fickle and darts from thought to thought, and I became fascinated by the patterns the raindrops traced down the window glass. Then the play of light and shadow drew me to the walls, where I found myself pulling at the torn edge of the wallpaper. Like most squats, damp had got into the room at some point in the past and the top layer peeled away to reveal another layer below—a vertical floral design in red, purple and green on a pale background. Carefully I stripped a couple of square feet away. And, while behind me Lilith howled obscenities in the throes of her passion, I started on the next layer. This revealed a faded leaf design in silver and turquoise. The colours pulled at me and I realised that if I could just find the original surface I might open a portal to another dimension—one of style and colour and exquisite taste.

But I had to be patient. Clawing the walls would disrupt the delicate lines of cosmic energy that flowed along the pinstripes of the layer of blue linen-finish paper. Delicately, I peeled a loose corner until I uncovered a beautiful mustard yellow bird that glowed with an inner light. Gently and meticulously I revealed more. A trellis design overgrown with olive and brown brambles sporting red flowers and crimson birds. I knew it at once as a classic design from 'the Firm', the company founded by William Morris to bring back craftsmanship to a world turned grey and smoky by the Industrial Revolution.

I was ready for a hallucination then and willed my mind into the pattern in front of me, but nothing happened. The wallpaper shone out of the hole in the wall, the light shifting like sunlight through a real trellis, real branches and real birds, but that achingly rational part of my brain stayed aloof. Chemistry, it said, it's all chemistry.

At some point Nigel escaped the bed and fled whimpering into the cupboard and closed the door behind himself.

The trellis and its mustard-coloured birds mocked me from the wall.

'I think we're sinking,' said Merton, for what I realised was the third or fourth time.

I was still coming down and it took concentration to focus on Merton, who was stark naked and pacing up and down at the foot of the bed. Lilith was sprawled face down, arms and legs spread like a starfish to occupy as much space as possible. There was no sign of Nigel, and in my elevated state I seriously gave consideration to the thought that Lilith had devoured him following coitus.

Merton rocked back and forth on the balls of his feet, as if testing his footing.

'Definitely sinking,' he said, and ran out the door.

I flailed about a bit until I found a packet of Lilith's Embassy Filters and a box of Swan Vestas, managed to not light the filter on the second attempt and dragged in a grateful lungful. A burst of head-clearing nicotine helped chase away the last of the lysergic acid diethylamide and I was just trying to determine whether I'd hallucinated a naked Merton when he reappeared.

'I've got good news and bad news,' he said. 'We're not sinking but we're definitely flooding.'

The cellar was divided into two parts. The stairs led down to the smaller part of it, essentially a wide corridor which used to house, so Nigel insisted on telling me, the coal chute—now bricked up. A big metal reinforced door opened into the larger part of the cellar—the part with over ten grands' worth of fabric stored in it. The door was closed but the corridor part was two inches deep in filthy water.

'Don't open the door!' called Nigel from the top of the stairs.

I had no intention of leaving the dry section of the stairs, let alone risking the cuffs of my maroon corduroy flares in what looked to me like sewage overflow. Merton, who'd been trying to force the door open, now splashed back as if stung. For a man who I'd once seen cheerfully batter a traffic warden for awarding him a ticket, it was odd how he never argued with Nigel—not about practical things to do with the house anyway.

Nigel, resplendent in a genuine Indian cloth kaftan—or so he claimed, passed me and stepped gingerly barefoot into the water. Reaching the door, he rapped sharply with his knuckles just above the waterline, then he methodically rapped up the door until he reached head height. After a few experimental raps to confirm, he turned to me and told me I was deader than a moleskin waistcoat.

'The whole room's flooded,' he said. 'Probably not a good idea to open this door.'

I sat down on the stairs and put my head in my hands. I did a mental inventory of what I'd stored and how it had been packed. It was bad, but if we could pump out the room half of it could be salvaged—especially the silks, since the individual rolls had been wrapped in polythene.

Thank God for Hans von Pechmann, I thought, and got to my feet.

'We need to drain the room,' I said. 'Nigel, get a pump and enough hose to run it back out to the river.'

Nigel nodded.

'Yeah, yeah,' he said, and practically skipped up the stairs.

'Put some clothes on before you go out!' I called after him.

I told Merton that when we had the pump and the hose, he would have to cut a suitable hole in the door—near the top.

'Will you need tools?' I asked.

Merton eyed up the door.

'I have what I need in my bedroom,' he said.

'Good,' I said. 'Let's have a cup of tea.'

* * *

It took Nigel the best part of the day to source the suitable equipment. In the meantime, I sent Merton out to the local phone box to see if I couldn't rustle up another life- and kneecap-saving transaction. Ideally, I should have been making the calls myself but I didn't dare show my face on the street—it's a well-known face, even in South London. I spent the time cataloguing my wardrobe, alas much reduced by my exile, ironing that which needed ironing and casting away those items that had fallen out of style since my last purge.

Some things never go out of style—some things, thank God, will never come back. Let us hope that the lime-green acrylic aquiline button-down cardigan is one of them. I really don't know what I was thinking when I bought it.

Apart from a spectacularly noisy toilet break, Lilith stayed blissfully asleep in the main bedroom until tea-time and then vanished into the bathroom for the next two hours.

Once Nigel had returned with the pump and the hose,

Merton used his hammer and chisel to cut a rough hole, six inches across, near the top of the door. Nigel had brought down the cream-coloured hostess trolley and mounted the pump on that to keep it out of the water. Once it was rigged we ran a hosepipe up the stairs, down the hall, across the kitchen and poked it out the back window. Merton stayed to supervise the outflow while I returned to the top of the stairs and gave Nigel the nod.

It looked ramshackle and was, indeed, held together with string and gaffer tape. But like most things that Nigel built, especially his improvised hookahs, it was perfectly adequate. The pump puttered into life, the pipe going through the hole in the door stiffened, there was a gurgling sound and I followed the passage of the water upstairs and into the kitchen. There, an arc of water shot from the hose and into the river beyond.

'How long until it's pumped out?' I asked.

'A couple of days,' said Nigel.

When I objected, he pointed out that it was a small-bore hosepipe, that the cellar was large and that we didn't know how the river water was getting in.

Some things you can't control, I suppose, such as Lilith—who I found sitting in the kitchen in a loose yellow kimono, drinking brandy and letting her assets hang out.

'It smells different in here,' she said.

I pointed out that the window was open to allow

egress of the hosepipe and was thus allowing fresh air, to which Lilith was generally unaccustomed, to enter the room. Lilith grunted and said she was going out that evening to meet some friends in Soho.

I tried to talk her out of it but she insisted, and there was no stopping Lilith when she was set on something.

'What if the Deplorables see you?' I asked.

'Darling,' said Lilith, throwing an orange ostrich feather boa around her neck, 'the Deplorables never frequent the places I do and in any case—I'm invisible.'

I was making another calming cup of tea when I realised that Lilith had been right. The kitchen smelt fresh and, oddly, sun dappled—if you thought sun dappled was a smell. I went to the open window and took a deep breath. Not normally something I'd recommend given the foetid nature of the river—which still looked more like a canal to me—behind the house. The air was fresh and another thing I noticed was that the water shooting out of the hosepipe was clear. I pulled the pipe in a bit and had a closer look and then an experimental taste— just the tip of the tongue, you understand. It was plain, clean water. Perhaps, I thought, the cellar had been flooded by a burst mains pipe. If so, then there was a chance that much of my stock might survive relatively intact.

I also noticed that the house had a small back garden, or rather a side garden, an overgrown patch of weeds and brambles that filled a roughly triangular space between next door's garden wall, the river and the side of the kitchen. I replaced the hose and went looking for the door that led to the garden. I'm not a horticulturalist myself, but to a man in my position, knowing there's a back door—for egress in extremis—is always a comfort.

It took three days to drain the cellar, which passed as quickly as two quarters of Lebanese cannabis resin could make it. Now, I've never been one to get the munchies, but Nigel could consume an astonishing amount of fish and chips, and poor Merton was forced to make several supply runs. On the morning of the fourth day, Nigel declared that we could force the door and I went to fetch Merton.

Who was nowhere to be found.

His room was as he always left it, the bed made with military precision and knife-edge creases. Merton was a thoroughly institutionalised boy, but what institution—the navy, prison, the Foreign Legion—I'd never thought to ask. His clothes, though dull, were hung or folded with the same admirable care. His tool case was missing but the canvas bag containing his baseball bat, bayonet and the long wooden stick with the stainless steel barbs that I didn't want to know the purpose of, was tucked into the wardrobe next to his two spare pairs of Doc Martens boots.

I returned to the basement corridor, which Nigel had

mercifully mopped clean once the muddy water had
soaked away. Nigel was standing by the door to the cellar, stock-still and staring at something on the floor.

'What is it?' I asked.

Nigel pointed mutely at a battered blue metal tool-
box sitting by the door. Its top was open and its trays
expanded to reveal its rows of neatly arrayed tools and
boxes of screws and nails.

'He must have gone inside,' said Nigel. His voice
dropped to an urgent whisper. 'Inside there!'

Since I had no idea why Nigel was so agitated, I
reached out and pushed the door open. It opened a frac-
tion and then pushed back—as if someone was leaning
against the other side.

'Merton,' I said, 'stop fucking about and let me in.'

I shoved harder and the door opened a crack and out
poured a weird sweet smell like cooked milk. And with
it a sense of outraged dignity which so surprised me that
I jumped back from the door, which slammed shut.

'Is he in there?' asked Nigel.

'Must be,' I said, but I wasn't sure I believed it.

Neither of us could match Merton—because that's
who it had to be—for physical might. I mean, I employed
him precisely because he could intimidate your average
creditor just by breaking wind. So we trooped upstairs
for a cup of tea and some pharmaceutical reinforcement.

'Got any more black beauties?' asked Nigel, who never

could separate his biphetamines from his common or garden amphetamines. I swear, you try to educate people but there are limits. I gave him a couple of ludes, and given the day we'd had so far, took a couple myself. Lilith returned, fabulously drunk at two in the morning, and we all piled into bed and didn't get up until the next afternoon.

The door to the cellar remained closed and Merton's tool case was still where he'd left it. I tried the door, but it was stuck fast with no give at all. I even tried knocking it down, like they do in the films, but all I did was bruise my shoulder.

If Merton was in there, he wasn't coming out until he was good and ready. And since I wasn't getting in, I had to accept that I wouldn't be realising any value from my stock of fabrics any time soon. Still, I'd already written down their value and put other deals in motion to generate cash flow—another drug deal, as it happens. A stack of Happy Bus LSD out of Rotterdam. A little bit riskier than my normal deals, but needs must as they say.

Without Merton, I was forced to rely on Nigel to go out and make the necessary phone calls. Unlike Merton, who followed instructions without question, I had to explain everything to him as if he were in a spy movie with Michael Caine. Once he had the gist, he darted out the front door wearing a RAF surplus greatcoat. As

I watched him go from the upstairs window, I realised that his hair had grown long enough to reach between his shoulder blades and I wondered why I hadn't noticed.

The next couple of days went past with no sign of Merton, and I only managed to keep anxiety at bay with the help of my dwindling supply of cannabis resin and long punishing nights with Lilith.

The door to the cellar remained closed.

When I had nerved myself up to go look, I noticed that something had been jammed into the cracks around the edge of the door—as if it had oozed out from inside the cellar in liquid form and then set on contact with air. I took a set of pliers from Merton's tool case and worried a fragment out. It's a long time since I've prepared a slide in earnest, but while I didn't have a microscope I did have a jeweller's glass I keep for checking crystal shape. Under magnification the fragment revealed itself to be a tangle of threads—blue cotton, my good Egyptian cotton at a guess. I picked at the tangle with a pair of tweezers and a strange notion struck me—that the threads weren't tangled randomly, that there was a pattern to the knots.

I could imagine a circumstance where the pressure of water could both shred the original weave of a cloth and then tangle the threads. I could even imagine water pressure forcing the threads around the edges of the door, but it seemed unlikely. Before I discovered fashion and pharmaceuticals, I did a degree in chemistry. Started a degree, to be precise—I stopped paying attention in the second year. But I'd always thought of myself as rational even when under the influence.

If I'd known what I know now, I would have run screaming from the house and taken my chances with the Deplorables. But I lived in a much smaller world in those days.

Although large enough for my Rotterdam connection to agree to a deal. Not only that, but it seemed my credit was good enough for me to procure a sample shipment on good faith. With the profit from that sale I could finance a larger shipment and thus dig myself out of my financial predicament and quit the squat—and its creepy basement.

The only catch being that I would have to provide my own mule to bring the sample in. Normally you don't use your friends as mules, not even friends of friends. What you really want is a gullible person who's been talked into it by someone you know only through business. I knew a guy who could meet a girl at a party one night and have her on a plane to Ankara the next day. He made a living recruiting mules and didn't mind some wastage at all—right up to the point someone's mother gave him both barrels of her husband's grousing shotgun. The police never caught her and only Merton and I turned up for the funeral.

* * *

It wasn't hard to persuade Lilith to fly to Rotterdam—especially first class—and the beauty was that wherever she touched down, she paid for herself. Or, to be strictly accurate, other people took care of her needs for her. The downside, of course, was that you had to allow her time to party—in this case, at least a week. You'd think without Lilith sharing the high thread cotton sheets of the four-poster I'd be getting more sleep, but I found myself spending most of every night staring at the underside of the bed's canopy.

It didn't help that I had to ration the Quaaludes—I needed them to keep Nigel functioning.

'There's something in the cellar,' he said, and refused to go down into the basement.

I, on the other hand, found myself increasingly drawn to the cellar door. Especially when it started to flower.

It started with a spray of cotton around the door frame, overlapping triangular leaves of white and navy-blue cotton that stuck to the bricks of the wall as if they'd been glued in place. I took a sample and found that instead of a regular weave, the cloth was formed by the intertwining of threads in a complex pattern. Some of the threads amongst the white and blue were a bright scarlet and spread through the fabric in the branching pattern of streams into a river basin. Or, more disturbingly, like capillaries branching out from a vein.

I did make an attempt, cautiously, to scrape one of the 'leaves' off the wall with a trowel I found in Merton's tool case. But even as I pushed the blade under the edge of the cloth I felt such a wave of disinterest—I cannot describe it more clearly than that—that I found myself halfway up the basement stairs before I realised what had happened.

The next day the cotton leaves had spread out at least another six inches and surrounding the door were tongues of crimson and yellow organza. Individual threads had begun to colonise the door proper—curling into swirling patterns like ivy climbing a wall. I spent an indeterminate time with my back to the opposite wall, staring at the patterns to see if I could spot them moving.

I wondered what it meant. Perhaps Nigel was right, and the Age of Aquarius was upon us and we had entered a time of miracles.

When I was upstairs I tried to put the cellar out of my mind and concentrate on plans for the future. I had fallen into drug dealing almost by accident and had always found it an easy and convenient way to keep myself in the sartorial fashion I aspired to. But if my run-in with the Deplorables was an indication of the future, then perhaps it was time to pack it in. A boutique of my own instead, one in which I could serve both as owner-manager and inspiration. Before, the merest thought of doing actual work, no matter how supervisory, had filled me with disgust but now… now it seemed attractive.

I didn't trust the feelings.

I needed out of the squat. I needed to be strutting down the King's Road or Carnaby Street. I wanted back out into the world, where I could be as dazzling and as splendid as the first acolyte of the goddess of fashion.

But you need working kneecaps to strut your stuff. And so I stayed where I was.

By the third day the door was completely obscured behind a tapestry of red, black and gold thread, and wings of cotton spread across the walls and ceiling. The organza had likewise spread and a third wave of pink and yellow damask now framed the doorway. By the sixth day the entire corridor was curtained in swathes of multicoloured fabric, so that it seemed a tunnel to a draper's wonderland.

I no longer dared leave the safety of the foot of the stairs and yet I still found myself walking down them three times a day to look. The urge to walk into its warm comforting embrace was terrifying.

On the seventh day, Lilith failed to return. I started to seriously worry on the eighth; on the ninth, I fell into such a despair that no amount of near pharmaceutical grade Drinamyl amphetamines could lift me from it. On the tenth, a postcard arrived with four jaunty pictures of a tram stop, a fountain, a town square, a gigantic statue of a man holding up the sky and Groeten uit Rotterdam written across the front.

On the back Lilith sent me love and kisses, explained that she'd met a splendid sailor or three and would be staying on in the Netherlands for a bit, but not to worry because she'd found a perfectly wonderful Spaniard to courier my product back to London. Thoughtfully, she'd written the travel and contact details of the Spanish courier on the postcard—in plain English.

With a heavy heart I sent Nigel out to pick up the package and when he failed to return I was not surprised.

We live in a universe constantly assailed by the forces of entropy. Nothing good, pure or beautiful can stand up to the relentless regression towards the mean, the dull and the shabby. A minority have always striven to be a beacon in the gloom, a constant source of inspiration to those around them. Some worked through medium of paint, or music, or literature, but I have sought to make myself the living embodiment of style and culture.

God knows it hasn't been easy.

But a man should always know when he has been beaten. That morning, as I sat in the kitchen futilely waiting for Nigel to return, I realised that the time, for me, was nigh. I went upstairs, stripped myself down to my underwear—not nylon and not frilly, thank you, Ray—and, after taking a deep breath to steel myself, donned a pair of brown corduroy trousers and a matching moleskin shirt. A pair of Hush Puppies and one of Merton's donkey jackets completed my transformation. I looked in the mirror—I was unrecognisable.

Stuffing the last of my cash reserves into my pockets, I headed for the front door. I paused by the basement door only long enough to ensure it was closed. From behind it came a noise that might have been a giant breathing, or water flowing, or shuttles running back and forth across lines of thread.

I shuddered and walked boldly out into the sunlight.

My plan was simple. Take the train to Holyhead, the ferry to Dublin and then, via a few contacts I still had, to America and freedom.

I didn't even get as far as Garratt Lane before I ran straight into Cutter. I tried to brazen it out but somehow he recognised me instantly and called out my name.

I turned, ran back to the squat, slammed the door behind me and went for the back door. There I could escape via the garden, over the wall and run for Wimbledon Park station.

But Lead Pipe was waiting in the kitchen, with a cup of tea on the go and the Daily Mirror open to the back pages.

'About time,' he rumbled when he saw me.

Three guesses where I went next.

I was down the stairs and into the basement corridor before I even noticed that the walls had grown a fringe that glowed with a soft golden light. I was prepared to throw myself frantically at the cellar door but I found it open. I ran inside with no brighter plan than to barricade myself inside and hope the Deplorables grew bored.

Inside, the cellar was a riot of colour. The walls were arrayed with purple organza and burgundy charmeuse, while sprays of a brilliant blue habotai framed cascades of fabric woven in a dozen colours—scarlet, yellow and green—into tangles of vines, leaves and flowers. Globes of light hung suspended from golden threads in each corner, illuminating a bundle of gold and black embroidered silk suspended from tendrils of lace—like a cocoon from a spider's web.

Around me was a giant's breathing and the warp and weft of a loom gigantic enough to weave the stars themselves. I could no more have stopped myself from grasping that bundle than I could have stopped myself breathing.

The bundle was warm and squirming in my arms. I unwrapped a layer of gauzy chiffon, gazed down on my fate and was lost.

'Oi,' said a voice from behind me.

I turned to find myself confronting the sartorial disaster that were the Deplorables en masse. I won't describe their appearance on the off chance that children may one day read this account.

'Can I help you, gentlemen?' I asked, because politeness is always stylish.

'Yeah,' said Cutter. 'You can give us the ten grand you owe us.'

'Plus interest,' said Lead Pipe.

'Plus interest,' said Cutter.

'I'm rather afraid I haven't got it,' I said.

'That's a shame,' said Cutter, and he turned to Lead Pipe. 'Isn't that a shame?'

'It's definitely a shame,' said Lead Pipe.

The bundle in my arms squirmed a bit and made happy gurgling noises.

'Since the money is not forthcoming, I'm afraid we'll be forced to take measures,' said Cutter. He looked once more to Lead Pipe. 'Is your sledgehammer ready?'

By way of reply, Lead Pipe held up his sledgehammer and I couldn't help but notice that there were brown stains on the long wooden handle.

'And Gnasher,' said Cutter. 'Do you have a marlinspike about your person?'

Gnasher grunted and held up a pointed lump of metal that I can only presume, in my ignorance of all things nautical, was a marlinspike.

Cutter turned back to me and smiled nastily.

'I'd say that you should take this like a man,' said Cutter. 'But that would be a waste of time.'

Never mind his rudeness, I had more pressing concerns.

'Shush,' I said. 'You'll wake the baby.'

Cutter's face suffused to a fine shade of puce and he opened his mouth to continue his ranting, so I twitched aside the fine damask sheet to reveal my daughter nestled in her bundle of silk and high thread Egyptian cotton.

Her beautiful brown face broke into a charming smile and, opening her chubby arms in a benediction, she laughed—a sound like water tumbling over stones.

Cutter gave me an astonished look and whispered.

'Is this your ...?'

'Yes,' I whispered back. 'Her name is Wanda.'

'But,' said Cutter, 'you can't keep her here.'

'She likes it here,' I said indignantly.

'It's a dump,' said Lead Pipe in a low rumble. 'It's not fit for human habitation.'

'He's right,' said Cutter. 'There's damp and mould and the kitchen is a disgrace.'

'And there's no nursery,' rumbled Lead Pipe.

'And the garden is a jungle,' said Gnasher. 'Totally unsuitable.'

'Gentlemen,' I said, 'I can't attend to any of these details if you break my legs.'

'Obviously, we have to deal with the immediate shortcomings of this house before we return to the matter of breaking your legs,' said Cutter. 'Don't we, boys?'

'I know a couple of builders,' said Gnasher. 'And Lead Pipe has green fingers. Ain't that right?'

Lead Pipe cracked knuckles the size of walnuts.

'That's true,' he said.

'Really?' I said.

'You should see his allotment,' said Cutter. 'He has compost heaps you wouldn't believe.'

I thought of the rumours of what exactly happened to people who crossed the Deplorables, and I decided that I actually did believe in those heaps.

'About my legs,' I said, but Cutter wasn't listening.

'And there's the roof,' he said, and the others nodded.

'About my legs,' I said louder and then wished I hadn't, because the trio were jerked out of their dreams of home improvement and focused on yours truly in a somewhat disconcerting manner.

'What about them?' asked Cutter, taking a step towards me.

'I thought we might reach a more mutually beneficial arrangement,' I said.

'What kind of beneficial arrangement did you have in mind?' he said.

'There's the matter of the way you dress,' I said.

Cutter pushed his face towards mine.

'What's wrong with the way we dress?' he said. 'It's practical.'

'Stain resistant,' said Lead Pipe

'Yes, but,' I said, 'it could be so much more.'

And Wanda laughed again and this time behind the chuckling stream was the crisp snap of fabric shears and the whistling hum of the shuttle as it plays back and forth across the thread.

'But first,' said Cutter, waving a blunt finger in my face, 'we have to sort out the playroom.'

* * *

And that was that. I gave up the pharmaceutical trade and opened a boutique instead. Cutter and his boys were my first customers, and while they never stopped being an unsavoury gang of foul-mouthed thugs, at least when they broke legs they were well dressed while doing it.

Merton, it turned out, had fled the squat the day we pumped out the water and, being in need of some security, assaulted a police officer so that he could spend a couple of nice peaceful years at Her Majesty's pleasure. Lilith visited him regularly, and after he got out they ran an animal sanctuary just outside Abergavenny until their deaths, within three months of each other, in 2009. Nigel is still alive and taught cybernetics at

Imperial College until his retirement a couple of years ago.

My daughter and I never got around to giving the boutique a name. It was always just 'the shop' and given that we never advertised, it's a wonder we stay in business. We're always at the cutting edge of fashion. We were out of flares while the Bay City Rollers were still number one and stocking bondage trousers before John Lydon had dyed his hair. We've moved the shop a couple of times and, while we're hard to find, we're always close to the river.

So if you want to know what the herd are going to be wearing next spring, and if you can find us and are prepared to pay the price, you too can join the ranks of the stylish, the à la mode, and truly become a dedicated follower of fashion.

Favourite Uncle

(*Set between* The Hanging Tree *and* Lies Sleeping)

Introduction

Abigail is one of those characters whose first appearance was supposed to be limited to a paragraph or three but who, once created, refused to leave the narrative. Since making her debut as annoying local teenager in *Moon Over Soho*, she then graduated to plucky teenaged side-kick by *Broken Homes* and is now on track to have her own novella, *What Abigail Did That Summer*, coming soon.

We used to be friends—a long time ago.

We went to the same primary but she went to Parli and I went to Burghley and that's like a whole quantum level of separation. And for your information I know what the word quantum actually means—actually. So given the difference in our energy states it was going to take a bit more than some fuzzy feeling to bridge that gap. That's why it was a bit of a shock when I walked out of school after Latin club and found her waiting for me in front of the school gate. Her in her Parliament Hill School uniform and everything.

'Hey Abi,' she says.

'Hi Babs,' I say. Her real name was Barbara Wilson but I've called her Babs since infants and I'm not about to stop just because she's a head taller than me.

'I need your help,' she says.

'My help?'

'Yeah,' she says. 'Natalia said that you were the one to go to for things.'

'Natalia?'

'She said you got her out of the house in Hampstead,' said Babs. 'Whatever that was about.'

One of the kids from that… incident. They were supposed to be sworn to secrecy. I told Peter he was wasting his time, but it's not like we have a convenient obliviate spell to do the job for us.

Babs looks down at me hopefully.

'She said you could help,' she says.

'Fine,' I say. 'What's the problem?'

'I don't think my Uncle Stan is really related to me,' she says.

'Okay,' I says.

Babs shifts from foot to foot.

'And I think he's over a hundred years old,' she says as if that explains everything.

'Step into my office,' I say.

* * *

'What you've got to understand about Uncle Stan is that we only ever see him at Christmas,' says Babs over a hot chocolate in the Café de la Paix.

I use this café because it's halfway up Fortess Road and so is convenient for school without being so close that I have to put up with year eights getting in my business.

'Every year he arrives like the day before Christmas, stays with us until two days later and leaves,' says Babs. 'He sleeps in my room, which means I have to share with my brothers, which is bare dry.' She blinks and looks at me. 'How's your brother?'

Why can't people look things up on Wikipedia and know what a stupid question that is? They've always got to ask and what am I supposed to say? He's worse, he's going to keep on getting worse, and then he's going to die.

Before I'm old enough to do anything about it.

'About the same,' I say.

'Yeah, sorry about that,' Babs says. 'Anyway, like I was saying, he stays in my room.'

'Does he bring presents?' I ask.

'What?'

'It's Christmas,' I say. 'Does he bring presents?'

'I don't know,' says Babs. 'Is that important?'

I say it might be, and Babs says that all the presents from everyone go under the tree and she doesn't always check the labels when she opens them. I'll bet she doesn't. I'll bet she rips off the wrapping too, as if you couldn't do it neatly and save the paper for something else.

'Does he touch you?' I ask—because sometimes you've got to ask, don't you? Saves time.

Babs makes a disgusted face.

'Nothing like that,' she says. 'That's not what the problem is at all.'

The problem being that they had done a project at school about tracing your family tree. Babs, being Babs, dutifully persuaded her dad to invest in one of those genealogical apps that does most of the work for you and sets about finding out who her great grandparents were and all that.

Mine, in case you're wondering, are half from Sierra Leone and the other half are a lot of genuine cor-blimey cockneys and Irish—Catholic and Protestant, it's not as uncommon as people think.

My dad being African, it wasn't as if randomly attaching non-biological aunts and uncles was without precedent.

'I asked my mum whose uncle he was. She said she didn't know, but she remembered him coming to Christmas when she was a girl,' says Babs.

'So he's on your mum's side of the family,' I say, and she's really got my interest now.

'I suppose so,' says Babs. Her mum had been born in Harrogate and had come down to London for university where she'd met Babs's dad who'd originally come from Newcastle. They stayed in London, got married and bought a house in Tufnell Park back when houses were cheap. There they had Babs's two older brothers and then Babs—I remember that house. She had a big bedroom all to herself and the most toys—I was bare jealous.

'The thing is,' says Babs. 'I can't find a single photograph of him.' Not even when she'd opened up the albums from the Dark Ages and the faded Instamatics had become actual black and white pictures.

I tell her that I charge ten quid a day plus expenses and thirty up front, and she doesn't even quibble—told you she was loaded. Plus she has to give me her log-in details for the genealogical app.

She hesitates, which is sensible, I wouldn't want other people to know my family history either.

'Save time, won't it?' I say.

* * *

I am sitting in the mundane library at the Folly with a pile of books, my A4 research notebook and one of Molly's experimental cakes. The notebook is from Paperchase and has an orange cover with a skinny white woman drawn on it—I only bought it because it has squared paper, which I prefer. The books are all those in the library whose index cards list immortality and calendar related events. There are fifteen books in total, ranging from Kingsley's 'On Fairies and Their Abodes' to Heston Chalmers's 'Index of Faerie Volume I'. The Chalmers is well frustrating because Volume 1 only goes from A to D and he never finished any of the other volumes. I know there's got to be notes somewhere and one day I'm going to make Professor Postmartin go find them.

The cake is a pecan and apple sandwich—it smells really good—but I'm leaving it because I'm being strong. If you want to do magic you've got to rise above the body—you've got to keep a clear head.

I'm reading Hiddlestone's *Miscellanea* which, while not what you'd call useful, is at least good for a laugh. He says that there are reports that some men, 'Have extended their existence by accident rather than design. These unfortunates, for such I judge them to be, show little understanding of their plight and when questioned seem strangely insensate of the peculiarity of their circumstances. How these wretches came about their unfortunate state is still a mystery to the frustration of those amongst us who seek a magical cure for ageing.'

There follows a long boring paragraph where Marcus Hiddlestone goes off on one about the quest for immortality. He's pretty certain that God allots a set time for every man—he never seems to mention women—and that it's futile to strive for more than what God gives you. Mr Hiddlestone and I are just going to have to disagree on that point.

I am staring into space and thinking of the jazz

vampires that Peter doesn't know I know about. Three women who became sort of immortal when they got bombed in a nightclub during World War Two. They were supposed to feed on jazz, or sex, or both, and didn't seem to know what they were either.

So if you can have white women who feed off jazz, why not an old man who feeds off… what? Christmas? Happiness? Mince pies?

I remember that the jazz vampires had victims. The musicians they fed on suffered physical damage. So I add 'Chk Fam Med Hist' to my action list. And then I add 'sauce FthXmas?'

I wonder whether I should ask Peter about the jazz vampires but decide not to. I don't want him taking an interest and stopping my investigation. The boy thinks I'm made of glass.

Assuming that it's just the one guy, does he only appear at Christmas? Just because Babs's family only see him once a year doesn't mean he doesn't visit other families for other holidays. He could be a peripatetic avatar of good cheer.

'Peripatetic' makes me laugh as I say it out loud. I taught it to my dad the other week and now he uses it all the time. He says working the railways is peripatetic because they're always moving around.

I spend another three hours making notes until I'm sure I've at least skimmed everything relevant. The only other useful thing I find is a note in the margin of the Charles Kingsley, on the passage about certain fae 'adopting' families at Easter and Christmas. Dickens' *Christmas Carol*?

Then I eat the cake while I think about what I've discovered.

The cake is special—crisp and tart, and other words they use on the Great British Bake Off—which Molly would totally win if she entered. You can get spoilt eating at the Folly. No wonder Bev keeps Peter well exercised.

The books can only take you so far, says Peter, because the Folly's always been big on theories and short on corroboration. But it's good to get that stuff sorted in case you start to see patterns in the evidence. But for evidence I'm going to need Wi-Fi so I pack up my things and head for the tech cave.

It's about five metres and a two hundred years from the back door of the Folly proper to the first floor of the coach house where Peter stashes all his tech. He's out on a shout today, so I reckon I've got a couple of hours to myself.

Peter's tower is better than my current laptop so I boot it up and, after disabling his keylogger, log into Babs's genealogy account. The immediate family is as I remember it. Mum, Dad, Babs, older brothers. Her parents are both the eldest of their siblings, so there are two aunts and three uncles—all but two of which live in London. Or, more precisely, in various dodgy postcodes beyond the North Circular.

I call Babs, saving my minutes by using one of Peter's backup disposables, and ask her whether any of her uncles and aunts routinely comes over for Christmas.

'You're joking,' says Babs. 'All of them.'

'What, every year?'

'Yeah,' she says. 'And all their kids too. It's like a total zoo.'

'Even the ones that live up north?'

'Them too.'

I hang up and check the chart.

Every living member of the family attends Christmas.

I think that's pretty special, and not just because none of them have killed one of the others yet. It's like totally unnatural. I mean, there's happy families... but this is totally ridiculous.

I'm feeling jealous. Proper envy—this is not helpful.

I do some routine clean-up on the genealogy chart to calm myself down.

Uncle Stan had a box all to himself. No surname, no date of birth, and no connections to any other member of the family. I believe I have, as Nightingale would say, exhausted all the possibilities of that particular technology.

Although there were some details of Babs parentage

that would be good for a laugh if I wasn't bound by a strict code of client confidentiality.

My phone rings and it's Mum. She tells me that Paul's condition has deteriorated and that he's going into hospital again. She wants me to pick up a takeaway supper for Dad so he's fed when he gets back from work that evening. He's working on the Overground which is closed for the weekend for engineering work.

She doesn't say where the money's coming from, because she knows I'm going to blag it off Molly—she's thrifty that way, is my mum. She once told me that some people get to be precious about their dignity, but not families like us—we've got to take any opportunity we can get. Mum and Dad see the Folly as my big chance, even though they have no fricking idea what that chance is.

I'd let it worry me, but dinner is dinner, and Molly does like to cook.

* * *

I'm walking into Great Ormond Street Hospital, where everybody knows my name—I've been coming here since before I can remember. I used to love coming here when I was a little kid and didn't know any better. It never scared me, everyone was nice to me and it was full of interesting stuff. I remember how big and solid the oxygen cylinders seemed and my dad telling me about the do's and don'ts of high pressure gas storage. There were machines and tubes and devices to look at and, when it was sunny and I was older, they let me go over the road to Coram Fields.

I'm here to visit my mum because when Paul comes to hospital it's because there's a problem and he's either asleep or away being scanned or something. I walk past a couple of white girls sitting in adjacent beds, one with no hair and a tube up her nose. They're both smiling.

There are balloons and tinsel and Father Christmas. The first of this year's surprise celebrity Santas have already passed through leaving presents and photo-opportunities behind them.

A junior oncologist from Brazil once told me that the reason cancer is lethal in children is because young bodies are so full of life. That's how he said it, that their cancers are full of life too. But, he said, because they are full of life children often defy your expectations and make miraculous recoveries.

'There's always hope,' he said.

Except when there isn't—I've learnt to be practical about this stuff.

Both Paul and Mum are asleep so I settle into the other chair with my sample GCSE Latin exam questions and wait for one of them to wake up.

* * *

I don't take chances with Christmas, and I generally start negotiating for what I want around Easter so I can wear my dad down over the course of the year. It has to be my dad because my mum is wheedle-proof—years of dealing with Paul, I guess. Still, I think she's the one who makes sure the presents are wrapped and stuffed into a pillowcase hanging off the end of my bed.

I wake Christmas morning from a dream in which me and Molly are presenting the Great British Bake Off, only Molly keeps missing her cues and the producer, who looks and sounds just like Nightingale, is just on the edge of a nervous breakdown.

I know from the quiet that Mum had already left for the hospital and Dad is on shift. He nearly always works Christmas Eve into Christmas Day. For the railways the holidays are mainly a golden opportunity to get some work done without all those annoying passengers getting in the way.

They didn't used to leave me on my own like this, but I'm big now and they trust me not to burn the house down.

I unpack the pillowcase they've left at the end of my bed and sit cross-legged on my bed with the presents arranged around me. I recognised the big soft badly-wrapped parcel as being from Aunty Rose and it will be clothes—it's always clothes. Brand new and not stuff I would ever wear, and not going to fetch much on eBay. I usually keep them in my wardrobe for a couple of years and then hand them back to Aunty Rose to send to Sierra Leone—I wonder if she notices?

There are various presents from Mum's family, which can be pretty hit and miss. Last year they clubbed together to get me a Purple Diamond vanity case which arrived full of makeup that was, shocking I know, all the wrong shades. Still I traded the make up at school and keep the case to house my specimen collection kit.

And some of the Mac cosmetics that Bev gave me later.

This time it's a single Christmas card, depicting a robin on a Christmas tree, containing an Argos Gift Card—no mention of how much is on the card, just Merry Xmas and a list of familiar names. They all signed their names separately so the card is going in the permanent collection.

I save the best for second from last. It's a heavy rectangle containing the main present—the one I've been pushing for since June. And yes it's a reconditioned Chrome Book with all the trimmings.

There's the usual bits and pieces at the bottom of the pillowcase, sweets, chocolates and shiny things from the market and the Pound Shop. I sort them into edible, swappable and recyclable.

I open the last present—the one from Paul. It's a small box shape and wrapped in silver paper.

I always get a present from Paul. My mum swears blind that Paul helps her choose them, though we both know that hasn't been possible for years. Still, last year it was a hand-carved statue of a cat—not something my mum would choose on her own.

I carefully remove the paper to reveal a watch box. Inside is a Hamilton Officer's watch with a black face and a really kruters khaki strap. But I don't care because it's a mechanical movement—it's for a practitioner who doesn't want her own magic messing with her timepiece. It's a wizard's watch.

I wind it up, set the time and slip it onto my wrist.

Then I cry for a bit because it's the best present I've ever got.

* * *

I am standing outside Bab's house on Dalmeny Road just off Tufnell Park Road. It's one of those big old semis with a side passage to the back garden and a staircase that goes up to the front door. There is a holly wreath carefully fastened around the brass door knocker. There's also an old fashioned round doorbell which I press. It goes ding dong and through the door I hear voices asking whether anyone is expecting anyone.

Me and Dad visited Paul and Mum at the hospital and had Christmas dinner there. My dad says that Great Ormond Street has the best food of any hospital in the country. He's been awake for twenty four hours by the time we leave, but it doesn't show until he gets home. I leave him snoring on the sofa while I head up Tufnell Park to finish the case.

I am nervous because there are lots of voices and I only know Babs. Peter knocks on strange doors all the time and says the trick is to remind yourself you are there for a good reason.

'But what if you can't tell them, because it's a secret?' I asked him.

'That's alright,' he said. 'They don't need to know the reason—only you need to know.'

A tall white woman in a mauve jumper and tan slacks opens the door and looks down on me. She has blue eyes and brown curly hair —Peter's taught me to notice things like that—with a silver paper crown crammed on top. Her face is flushed and she looks both happy and surprised to see me.

'Good god,' she says. 'Is that you, Abigail? Come in, come in. You're so grown.'

She pulls me into the house. I can smell turkey and roast potatoes and sprouts and coal smoke. So maybe not just smell because later I check and find they have a fake real fire in the living room—the kind with concrete logs and a gas flame. I've missed Christmas dinner, she says but they're playing games and the more the merrier.

They've got one of those houses with the front room knocked through to the back room to make one large space. The front half has the sofas and the TV and the dog, a particularly stupid looking Labrador called Pom Pom. The walls are light brown and between the fire, the candles ranged along the mantelpiece and the art-fully positioned strip lighting, it is bright and cosy and glittering. It's also stuffed with Babs's family… well, all those over the age of thirteen. The younger kids are upstairs in Babs's brother's bedroom playing on her PS3.

There's her dad's brother Stephen, who is going through a messy divorce and is expected to lose his house, his beloved Mercedes and access to his kids. He stands in the centre of the room wearing a paper hat and a grin and opening his hands to indicate that it's a book.

'It's a book,' yells Babs's mum's sister Beatrice, who works as a dinner lady at a works canteen in Barnsley and who has a son that came within one sentencing guideline of youth detention for twocking a Prius in Halifax town centre last April. He is sitting at his moth-er's feet, a smile on his face and also, I notice, a can of Special Brew in his hand.

They're all there, the sisters and the brothers and the spouses and children. Pink cheeked and jolly in the light of the fake fire, and I can feel something occult coming off them in waves like the smell of plum brandy and mince pies.

And a quiet space behind me—a still spot.

I turn and look back towards the dining room end of the room, where shadows collect around a seated figure.

I look over at Babs, who is perched on the arm of a sofa. I try to catch her eye but she is far too busy with second syllable. Sounds like… banana? Monkey? Ape? Sounds like ape!

I wonder if I'm in danger, but I think not.

I wander over.

'Come in, come in, young lady,' says Uncle Stan, 'and know me better.'

He is a skinny old white man whose neck seems too small for his shirt collar and his ears and nose too big for his face. Still has a thick head of hair, gone grey and brushed back from his forehead. I swear his eyes were the darkest brown I've ever seen on a white guy in my life.

He waves at a chair opposite him.

'Come, come, lass and know me better,' he says and I sit down.

The dining table is a No Man's Land of pillaged chocolate boxes, unexploded crackers, empty bottles and forlorn buttresses of spun sugar icing.

As I get closer, I smell holly and pine needles and wood smoke and decide that my estimate of Uncle Stan's age was out by hundreds of years. Maybe thousands. Peter would have had a fit if he knew I was sitting down with somebody this magical. Mind you, Peter is shagging a river goddess so he's one to talk.

'So, you're Uncle Stan,' I say, because a positive identification solves problems later.

He smiles. A warm smile, where the good humour goes all the ways to his eyes, but in those eyes I think I can see something else—but I don't know what.

'That's what they call me,' he says.

'Good,' I said and poke him with the poker I'd borrowed from the set beside the fireplace. It's not hot or nothing, and I don't poke him hard—just enough to make sure he's physically there.

A sort of light flares in his eyes—not a real light, I guess, with real photons, but something that my brain is interpreting as a flash. His smile grows broader and I fight down an urge to lean away.

'Good for you,' he says. 'Have a crème egg.' He pushes over a bowl filled with Cadbury Creme Eggs. 'The mother buys them just after Easter when they're going cheap and brings them out at Christmas.'

'That's stupid,' I say before I can stop myself.

'Is it?' said Uncle Stan. 'Why's that? Chocolate is chocolate, after all.'

Sometimes a stupid thought comes out your mouth even when you know it's a stupid thought. 'Because it's for Easter, innit?' I say.

He offers me an egg again and I say no again.

He said there was no obligation, but I said I don't like the squidgy stuff inside.

'It started when they were a young family—a way to save money,' said Uncle Stan.

There was a high pitched giggle from the centre of the room as Babs makes a weird face to sell the mime. The rest of the family laughed, too loudly. The mother actually kind of hoots like a monkey.

I ask Uncle Stan if all this jollity was his doing.

He waves his hand in a disparaging gesture.

'I encourage a feeling of safety,' he says. 'People are less inhibited when they feel safe.'

'How long have you been visiting?'

'I've been coming down to London for Christmas since Barbara was old enough to unwrap her own presents,' he says.

'And before that?'

'With her mother's mother family.'

'In Harrogate.'

'Of course.'

'So you move about?'

'I'm peripatetic,' he says and smiles with enormous good humour.

'What's so funny?

'They talk about you,' he says.

'Who does?'

'The Parliament of Foxes gossip about nothing else,' he says. 'And on the edges of the horse fairs and carnivals from Appleby to Goldsithney they pass your name from hand to hand in the hope of guessing the future.'

He's trying to distract me. Peter has warned me that when you push people in an interview they instinctively look for ways to deflect you. If Uncle Stan is looking to make the conversation about me then I must be pushing his buttons.

'So you've been to all these places?' I ask.

'As I said—peripatetic.'

Which makes me smile although I don't tell him why.

'Do you visit other families?' I ask.

'Occasionally.'

'For Christmas?' I ask, in case he's some kind of weird multiple manifestation—don't laugh. It's totally possible.

'There are other celebrations than Christmas, other religions and beliefs, other moments of joy where people gather,' he says, and I smile.

'Joy?' I ask. 'Is that what you feed on?'

His eyes narrow but the smile doesn't fade.

'You're a clever little one,' he says. 'The foxes obviously don't know the half of it.'

I look back to where Babs's family are doing their Marks and Spencer Christmas advert impression.

'Does it hurt them?'

'Not at all,' he said.

'Why not?'

'You people are so profligate with your gifts,' he says and I note both the word 'profligate' and the use of 'you people'. Meaning he thinks he's a different people from me and Babs and the rest of us Homo sapiens. I wonder what are the chances of me getting a viable DNA sample from Stan and what favour I might extract from Dr Walid in exchange.

Babs is suddenly shouting 'Yes yes yes.' And fist pumping—obviously this family takes their charades seriously.

'Joy rolls off them like a mist,' says Uncle Stan. 'You cannot take what is freely given.'

'You can con people out of stuff though, can't you?' I say.

'But I don't need to,' he says. 'Do I?'

Maybe not. But nobody actually lives off joy. And while the jazz vampires thought they were eating jazz, what they were really doing was sucking the magic out of people's bodies. As far as I could tell from my research, Babs's family lived and died and got sick pretty much like everyone else. If Uncle Stan was shortening their lives I hadn't seen any evidence. Not that that was going to stop me from asking Dr Walid to do an epidemiological study. Just as soon as I could think of a reasonable excuse that didn't involve me admitting I'd been cavorting with dangerous supernatural types.

Still, I have questions.

'What about magic?' I ask.

'The same,' says Uncle Stan. 'Except for the likes of you.'

'The likes of me?'

'Them that wrap themselves in their own magic and wear it like a cloak.'

I need to go away and have a proper think, but I want to make sure that Uncle Stan is available for round two.

'Do you like this family?' I ask.

'Oh yes,' he says. 'They're my favourite.'

'Would you like to keep coming here?' I ask.

'How could you stop me?' he asks, so I give him the eye. To be fair, he lasts longer than Nightingale does when I use the eye on him. Only my mum can resist the eye, and she ain't here.

He sighs and raises his hands in mock surrender.

'So what do you want, young lady?' he says, sounding slightly annoyed.

'Tomorrow is Boxing Day,' I say. 'And I want you to get up nice and early while this lot are still snoring and come down to the hospital with me.'

'To what end?'

'Then they can get to know you better can't they?' I say. 'And you can make them feel safe and joyful.'

He didn't frown or nothing, but he looked over at where Babs's family were resting between bouts of compulsory charades and topping up their drinks.

'Traditionally Boxing Day has been a day of rest,' he says. 'After all, Christmas can only come once a year.'

'Some of the kids in the hospital aren't going to make it to the next Christmas, are they?' I say. 'So I reckon they might as well get the next one in extra early—just to be on the safe side.'

He looks at me for a long time—and then he smiles.

Vanessa Sommer's Other Christmas List

(Set around the same time as False Value)

Introduction

Just like Abigail, Vanessa Sommer was supposed to be a one shot character, in this case the baffled local cop to Tobias Winter's magic savvy federal officer. It was all going well until I decided to call her Sommer... You can see the problem. Winter and Sommer—it's a series. So when it came time to write the short story that would go with my first novella set in Germany I asked myself—how would learning magic is real affect a bright, inquisitive detective like Vanessa?

The year that KKin Vanessa Sommer was seconded to the BKA's Abteilung KDA she returned to her home village with two Christmas lists rather than one. The first list was the usual one, that she had started the previous January, which included reminders of what to buy her parents, her older brother, her younger brother, his wife, their toddler and all the cousins under the age of eleven. Over the course of the year that list had been embellished with other family related chores such as making sure her parents hadn't succumbed to any email scams and had laid in enough fire wood for the winter. Despite having grown up in Eifel, her father had all the country instincts of a Berliner and her mother, who had grown up in Dresden, had actively avoided acquiring any.

Vanessa's second Christmas list was more recent and stemmed from her discovery, much to her surprise, that magic was real, some rivers had goddesses, and that some police officers—when properly authorised—were practising wizards.

It was already one of the hazards of being police that you became suspicious of the everyday. You didn't have to spend much time on the job before realising that professional criminals are comparatively rare and that crime is something committed by ordinary people. In fact, the worse the crime the more ordinary the people who committed them—most murderers kill only once, and not just because they're caught and imprisoned.

Discovering that there was a whole world of magic and the supernatural hidden in the everyday had only fuelled Vanessa's professional paranoia. And so, in order to set her mind at rest, she had decided to properly assess her old home. To this end she made a second list of spooky locations from her childhood and, suitably armed with both lists and a back seat full of presents, Vanessa turned her Dacia Duster off the landstraße and up the twisty switchback road to home.

Sommerscheid, population nine hundred and thirty -three, sat astride the Sommerbach: a tiny tributary of the Kyll, in the one wide spot in an otherwise narrow valley that snaked up into the wooded hills of the Sommerwald. Vanessa's father swore blind that the village had its origins as a secret bandit camp whose nefarious residents had discovered that it was more lucrative to harvest wood, honey and charcoal from the forest than to mug passersby. Not to mention the famous local game sausage called Sommerwurst, which was less a salami and more a wild-whatever we shot when hunting-wurst. Or the fierce homebrewed peach schnapps that, despite technically being illegal, was still drunk on special occasions such as, for example, it being the month of January.

While her father was proud to proclaim that they were descended from the original bandits, the village was primarily a dormitory for nearby towns, supplemented by a handful of farmers, forestry workers and the sort of people who like the feel of rural isolation without actually being more than an hour's drive from the nearest Lidl.

Vanessa drove up through the centre of the village, across the Sommerbach, around the market square and out the other side to where her family home squatted under a heavy red tile roof. Her mother's Audi was missing from the driveway so Vanessa stole her place next to her father's VW. He emerged from around the back as soon as Vanessa had parked and helped her inside with her bags.

'Have you found a place in Meckenheim yet?' he asked once they'd dumped the bags and exchanged hugs.

She said she'd found somewhere temporary and asked after her mother, who was finishing up some conveyancing work at the office in nearby Hillesheim. Her father had worked at the same office before leaving for a semi-retirement as the village lawyer and guesthouse manager. Vanessa took her stuff up to her old room which, for eight months out of twelve, was rented out to hikers, birdwatchers and whoever else thought getting lost in the woods was a fun time. Here she checked both her lists before going down to see if her father had any of that locally brewed peach schnapps stashed at the back of his wine cellar.

First thing the next morning Vanessa let herself out through the kitchen door, across the back garden and out the back gate, which opened out into one of the hiking trails that led up into the hills. She followed it for a hundred metres or so before turning off onto a barely discernible path that led down towards the Sommerbach. The path ended where the stream leapt out of a narrow gorge and fell into a deep pool before flowing more sedately down out of the forest and through the town.

The local kids had been swimming in it since forever. There had once been a tyre swing that her father swore had come from a Mercedes W186 that had belonged to a wealthy hiker who had walked into the Sommerberg one fine spring morning and never returned. Sheltered as it was, the air here was still and mild even in winter. Vanessa remembered it as a magical place, so she took a moment to see if she could sense the vestigia which is the signature of real magic.

Nothing.

At least nothing she was sure of.

The sound of rushing water which might have been the laughter of children…

…or merely a memory from past summers or, just possibly, the actual sound of the waterfall.

Vanessa sighed and looked around for somewhere to hang her offering. The tyre swing tree looked suitable, so she hung the peach schnapps in a plastic bag from a low-hanging branch. Then she wrote—Call me if you want to talk—on one of her brand new BKA business cards and carefully attached it to the handle using a clip she'd stolen from her father's desk.

Vanessa didn't need to look at the actual list to mentally check off—Propitiate possible local river goddess.

Next on the list was the cave.

It was hard to spot unless you knew the way. You walked down into a hollow choked with silver birch and bushes until you reached a cliff face where the entrance to the cave opened exactly in the shape of a screaming cartoon mouth.

Vanessa, like most of the village kids, had regarded the cave with a kind of exalted terror, simultaneously repelled and attracted by its mysterious depths. They used to dare each other to venture inside and time how long they lasted before running out screaming. Rumour was that the cave system was endless and that there were underground rivers and packs of albino rats that could strip you down to your bones in seconds.

It looked smaller to adult Vanessa, and its dangers more prosaic.

She closed her eyes again and, as she had been taught, let her mind go blank. Again she was disappointed—there was nothing supernatural about the cave. Or at least, she told herself, nothing that she could recognise. She briefly considered having a look inside, but only a fool goes into an unknown cave without a helmet, lights and having first informed colleagues of her plans and when she expected to get back.

Vanessa mentally ticked off Terrifying Cave and pushed her way through the dripping undergrowth and back down to the trail. Just as she reached it, she heard the sound of an approaching engine and, after a short wait, a mini-tractor came around the corner pulling a trailer full of Christmas trees.

She recognised the driver, a tall young man with overlong arms and legs and a lugubrious face. He was dressed in an orange waterproof jacket and had a green Tyrolean cap jammed tightly on his head.

Vanessa waved.

'Hey Fabian,' she called.

Fabian Grünewald pulled up and said hello. They'd been at school together and after exchanging polite inquiries about each other's families he offered her a lift down the hill. As she clung to the back of the tractor she asked about the Christmas trees.

The Grünewalds had a hectare up the valley by the Brinkerhoffs place. Fabian had initially tried running it as a 'cut your own tree' enterprise, complete with a stall selling mulled wine.

'But it was too far from the road,' he said. 'People couldn't be bothered to walk that far.' Now he harvested and sold them at the Christmas market—mostly to local families.

'You can have yours now if you like,' he said.

So Vanessa hopped off the tractor at the back gate of her parents' house and chose a suitable tree from the trailer.

'Are you coming down for the market?' asked Fabian.

'Absolutely,' said Vanessa.

Sommerscheid was too small to have a month-long Christmas market but managed a week, from the second to third weekends in December. The local farmers and associations set out stalls and the volunteer fire fighters' association, of which Vanessa's father was the president, provided the carousel which had pride of place in the open space between the old fountain and the bridge.

The carousel was the next item on the list. It was old, for one thing. At least a hundred and fifty years old. And, for another, had been found abandoned in the woods by villagers returning from the war in the terrible winter of 1919. It looked splendid when set up, the horses freshly touched up and the brass work polished and gleaming, but Vanessa had once seen it in its lair, in a shed behind the fire station. Disassembled it was a thing of rust and sharp metal corners, horses stacked and shrouded, the pipes of the automatic organ as silent as impaling stakes.

Watching it whir around to a mechanical rendition of Ode to Joy, Vanessa had to admit that her negative reaction to the dismembered carousel might have had something to do with her being eight at the time.

She remembered refusing from then on to ride on the thing and standing sullenly watching while her brothers were whisked round and round. She'd been in such a state of diffuse, unfocused rage that her parents were forced to dangle iced gingerbread before her eyes to distract her. Looking back, she couldn't determine what had caused her anger and the actual memory had degraded to the point where she wasn't sure if it was a true memory or just something she thought she remembered. This sort of thing had not been a problem before she started studying magic, she thought. Still, she made a donation to the fire fighters' fund and climbed aboard.

There was no active vestigia that she could detect, but she still thought the wooden horses' dead-eyed stares were creepy, so she bought some iced gingerbread hearts and set off to find Fabian's Christmas tree stall. There she recognised a couple of familiar faces from her teen years. Like Vanessa, most had migrated out of the village to far off places like Cologne, Hamburg and Hillesheim— which was just down the L26 and had its own cinema and everything.

Inevitably, they ended up in the Café Blau drinking coffee and moaning about their parents, just as they had when they were teenagers. It was so normal Vanessa could almost pretend that she hadn't seen a colleague conjure a light from nothing or met at least two genuine river goddesses and a young man with horns.

Which thought reminded her to check her phone for messages.

It was dark and cold by the time they broke up and she went home for supper with her parents. Her mother asked whether she'd been keeping up her harp practise and Vanessa dutifully held out her hands so that her callouses could be felt. They discussed whether her younger brother was going to deliver another grand-child that year or whether his poor wife had finally had enough. Over coffee her father asked about the Abteilung KDA.

'Complex and Unspecific Matters? Sounds a bit complicated,' he said, and Vanessa and her mother groaned simultaneously.

Later, when she went up to her room, she found a red and white enamelled plate on the bedside table filled with a heap of sweets and wrapped chocolates. She ate some while she sat up in bed and did the coursework the Director had assigned her. She hid what remained of the sweets in her suitcase so she wouldn't finish them all off in one go.

The next morning Vanessa's phone rang but she didn't recognise the number.

'Hello, Vani?' said a voice she did recognise.

'Is that you, Fabian?'

'The one and only,' he said. 'Did you know someone's hung a bottle of peach schnapps from a tree and stuck your phone number on it?'

'That was me,' she said.

'Any particular reason?' asked Fabian.

'It was an experiment.'

'What kind of experiment?'

'Do you want to drink it?' asked Vanessa.

'Do you want to share?'

'Sure.'

'Meet me at the rock at one,' said Fabian.

The rock was just that, a slab of something hard that stuck out of the hillside above the village. It formed a flat shelf upon which generations of Sommerscheid teenagers had sat to look down upon their homes and get blind drunk on whatever they could steal from their parents' liquor cabinets.

Because neither of them were teenagers anymore, Vanessa made sure to bring a round of sommerwurst sandwiches with her, some napkins, and a couple of plastic glasses. The rain had stopped midmorning and the sky had cleared to allow some chilly sunlight.

Fabian's hat was starting to bother Vanessa, and not just because a Tyrolean hunter's cap was a bizarre fashion statement for a young German. More because it was always jammed on tight, and he was careful never to dislodge it. The police side of her brain wanted to know what he was hiding.

Even so, she later doubted she would have done what she did if they hadn't already drained three quarters of the schnapps. Fabian peered at the bottle.

'Why do they make it out of peaches?' he said. 'It's not like anybody grows peaches up here.'

'It's one of those mysteries,' said Vanessa.

'One of what mysteries?'

'One of those,' said Vanessa. 'Like: why do you wear a hat all the time?'

'What's that got to do with anything?' asked Fabian in what Vanessa considered an overly defensive manner. 'You never used to wear a hat when we were kids,' she said. 'Come to think of it, your father never took his hat off either.'

'It's none of your business,' said Fabian and stood up. 'Never saw him without a hat,' she said.

'You've obviously lost your ability to handle alcohol,' said Fabian.

Vanessa stood up and, because she had to know, snatched Fabian's hat off his head. Fabian stared at Vanessa in speechless outrage and she stared back in astonishment.

'How long has it been like that?' she asked and held out the hat for him to reclaim.

'Since I was twenty,' snarled Fabian, and grabbed it back. 'Satisfied?' He jammed the hat on his head, hiding a hairline that receded all the way back, past his ears. 'It happened to my father as well.'

And, with that, he turned and strode down the path down to the village. Vanessa sighed, but you don't last long in the police without developing a thick skin. So she finished the schnapps before heading home.

'Why did you make poor Fabian take his hat off?' asked Vanessa's mother that night at supper. It turned out she'd been talking to Fabian's mother who had complained about Vanessa's strange behaviour. 'The poor boy is sensitive enough as it is. I thought you were friends.'

'It was a stupid notion,' said Vanessa.

'Oh yes?' asked her father. 'What notion was that?'

'It's too stupid to speak of,' she said but she knew this would only spark her father's curiosity.

'Oh, tell me,' he said. 'You used to come up with some wonderful nonsense.'

'Yes,' said her mother. 'We thought you were going to become a writer.'

'So what was it?' asked father.

'You'll laugh,' said Vanessa.

'We promise we won't,' said her mother and solemnly put her hand on her heart.

'I thought he might have horns,' said Vanessa.

Both her parents stared at her for a whole second before bursting out laughing.

'Horns!' said her mother.

'Horns!' said her father. 'The Grünewalds don't have horns.'

'The very idea,' said her mother.

'That would be the Brinkerhoffs from up the valley,' said her father. 'They're the ones that grow horns.'

Three Rivers, Two Husbands and a Baby

(Set some time after the next Peter Grant novel following False Value*)*

Introduction

This started as A Moment but quickly got so out of hand that it effectively became a short story. People are always asking me about what happened with the River Lugg after Peter and Beverley's foray into its waters in *Foxglove Summer*—I'm glad you asked…

I knew it was a mistake to have the Teme family at the wedding. Not that we invited them exactly, but we'd been warned that a visit was a possibility so I'd factored them into my contingency seating plan. I put them on the table separating my immediate family from Victor's family. We had a big marquee courtesy of the Young Farmers and so had plenty of room. That's one of the advantages of marrying a farmer—there's plenty of space for a marquee and parking on your own land. I also made sure that they shared the table with Peter, Nightingale and Beverley. This is what we call, in the Job, intelligence led contingency forward planning.

'Or what us farmers call the next six months,' said Victor, but I forgave him because he was having trouble with his poly tunnels.

Between the Teme family, my family, and Victor's friends up from London, I reckon the only reason the wedding went as smoothly as it did was because at least a quarter of the guests were police officers in full uniform.

Including a couple of senior ones that had obviously been told to attend by their community access focus groups with a view to improving West Mercia Police's profile amongst the LGBTQ community.

To be fair, their presence kept the junior ranks in line who, since they weren't allowed to be rowdy, kept a lid on everyone else. So the wedding went remarkably smoothly, apart from the one incident with Aunty Leda and that rogue swan and I've promised never to tell anyone about that.

The Teme sisters turned up in what Beverley assured me was their finest. Miss Tefeidiad wore a dress—an honour, Beverley told me—in pale yellow linen with a square cut neckline, a slim gold necklace and heavy-looking gold bracelets depicting intertwined snakes on each wrist. Her eldest daughter, Corve, came in sensible country tweeds and her youngest, Lilly, in full black goth regalia topped by a half a ton of silver jewellery—most of it stuck through parts of her body.

Anyway, we made it through the speeches, including the one by Victor's best man Tarquin—who claimed to be looking forward to following Victor's example and 'rusticating' himself once his city career was finished. This went down about as well as you can imagine with my family and the three quarters of my colleagues who don't harbour big city dreams. Since every pub and café in the county aspires to, or at least dreams of, earning a Michelin star, the food was of course fabulous and Victor had made a special point of showcasing his almost organic meat and veg. There was a noticeable drop in conversational volume as everyone dug in and we were all feeling suitably merry when the band started up.

Choosing the music had proved a long and complex operation where Victor and I were forced to consider the complex intersection of rural and urban, policing and farming, mundane and mystical tastes. So, how we ended up with Late September, Ludlow's one and only Earth, Wind & Fire tribute band I will never know. They dress like Motörhead but sing like the Motor City and, occasionally, Boney M. At our request they opened their set with their famous cover version of 'Rasputin' that goes on for eleven minutes.

Once the ice was sufficiently broken so that everyone below the rank of Chief Superintendent felt free to dance, I grabbed the closest non-alcoholic drink and staggered over to a chair next to Peter.

'That's not a bad sound,' he said.

We sat watching Victor and Beverley groove for a bit and then Peter asked me if I'd noticed anything unusual about the River Lugg recently. Victor's farm is bounded by the Lugg on its west side and Peter, inexplicably, always asks about it when we chat.

'Why are you so interested in the Lugg?' I asked.

Miss Tefeidiad, who was sitting at the same table, took notice and leaned in.

'Yes, Peter love,' she said. 'Why are you so interested?'

Peter gave her a dark look and sighed.

'There was…' he hesitated, 'an event.'

'Is that what we're calling it now?' said Corve, returning with a third slice of cake. 'I bet that's not what Bev calls it.'

I never did find out what Peter's interest in the Lugg was—although now that it's too late, I have my theories—because Victor dragged me out to dance and after that we got so drunk that we didn't have sex until late the next morning.

* * *

A year later Victor and I were walking, somewhat unsteadily, home from the Mortimer Cross Arms when we ran into the foxes.

Not normal foxes, mind you, but the big talking buggers that introduced themselves to me the month after Peter, Beverley and I rescued the missing Rushpool kids. Since then they've been tipping me off about everything from tractor thefts to county line drug deals. And in return I scrupulously enforce the Hunting Act (2004) which outlaws hunting with hounds. And feed them custard doughnuts from Morrisons.

We were crossing the bridge by the mill when one

of them jumped up on the parapet and cried—'All hail Dominic Croft, hail to thee Constable of the West Mercia Police.'

It was lucky I was too sloshed to whack it with my baton. I was about to tell it to piss off when a second jumped onto the parapet next to it.

'All hail Dominic,' it cried. 'Hail to thee Detective Sergeant.'

By that time Victor and I had sussed what was going on, so we waited, swaying slightly, for the third fox. Who arrived late—scampering along the parapet to join its mates. Who tutted loudly.

'Sorry,' it said and then, louder, 'All hail Inspector Croft—Geographic Commander Northern Herefordshire hereafter.'

'You let them watch the Fassbender again,' I said to Victor. 'Didn't you?'

'You were on lates,' he said. 'And they promised to be good.'

'Hail Dominic and Victor,' the foxes chorused, 'soon to be blessed above all other minor landowners in Herefordshire and the wider border regions.'

'What?' said Victor.

'Congratulations,' said the first fox.

I asked for what, which seemed to confuse the foxes.

'Nothing special happened this evening?' asked the second fox.

Victor gave this some thought.

'Well,' he said, 'the mushroom wellington was particularly fine.'

The foxes exchanged looks and the first one coughed.

'Sorry about this,' it said. 'Nothing to worry about, see you around.'

Then they scarpered.

'You said it was tonight,' we heard one fox say as they vanished into the darkness.

'I thought it was tonight,' said a voice in the distance.

'Obviously it isn't,' said the fox now much further away. 'Is it?'

We waited in a silence for a couple of minutes.

'How drunk are we?' asked Victor.

'Not that drunk,' I said, and with that we went home.

Nothing else happened after that, and since I was off shift the next day I lay in our big 'genuine farmhouse style' brass bed until the late hour of eight AM when Victor, who'd got up at five, called me on my mobile.

'Can you come down to the set aside field? ' he said. 'The one by the river.'

* * *

Victor has a set aside area which he has kept, despite the fact that the EU policy that set it up has been defunct for over a decade. The boundaries of several fields have been set back from the path of the River Lugg, creating a strip of uncultivated land varying between three to five metres wide. There insects buzz, amphibians croak and flowers, or possibly weeds, bloom. To give the rest of the fauna a look in, the talking foxes have agreed not to hunt there—the custard doughnuts are the price for that.

Victor says the new straight boundaries make the fields easier to work and he thinks there are voles living in the riverbank, although currently we haven't spotted one yet.

What we could spot was the naked child poking around the muddy bank with a stick. He was a boy, aged about two, pale skinned with a shaggy mop of black hair and, when he looked our way, blue eyes. He looked well fed and, apart from the mud, well cared for. He gave us both a little wave before turning away to squat down and dig the soft earth around a tree root.

I had a bad feeling about this—particularly when I remembered the foxes being accidentally prophetic the evening before.

'What should we do?' asked Victor.

'Let's keep an eye on him while I make a few phone calls,' I said.

The boy seemed perfectly content to poke around

where he was while I called up control to see if there were any missing children reported and asked to be informed if any were in the next few hours.

I looked up to find that the boy had dug a worm out of the soil and was holding it up to show us. Once he was sure he had our attention he dangled the worm over his open mouth and made as if to eat it.

I'm from a big country family with uncounted nieces and nephews who I've been 'volunteered' to babysit over the years so I know a teasing bluff when I see it, but Victor was an only child.

'Don't eat that,' he said and scrambled down the bank and plucked the worm out of the boy's hands. 'We need those to maintain the soil matrix.'

The boy immediately threw his arms around Victor's neck, forcing him to pick him up.

'So where did you come from then?' asked Victor.

The boy solemnly stretched out an arm and pointed towards the middle of the river.

I sighed and made the phone call I'd been putting off.

* * *

We got back to the farmhouse and found an ancient blue Land Rover parked in the yard. Inside, sitting round our kitchen table, were Miss Tefeidiad and her daughters, Corve and Lilly. They'd helped themselves to my Hobnobs I noticed but had made a big enough pot of tea for everyone.

'Let's be having you then,' said Miss Tefeidiad and reached out to pluck the child from Victor's arms. She handled him with brusque competence, checking fingers, toes, limbs and teeth in much the same way I've seen Victor check a lamb.

'Seems to be all there,' she said, and dumped him on a startled Corve.

'Whatever should we do with him?' said Corve.

'Isn't he your responsibility?' I asked.

'Well technically, maybe,' said Corve gingerly passing the boy to Lilly. 'This is a bit of a turn-up for us. In the old days we'd just let him get on with it.'

'Get on with what?' asked Victor.

'Being alive,' said Corve. 'It's not as if he's in any danger from animals and the like, and back then the people would know well enough to leave him be.'

'Not like now,' said Miss Tefeidiad. 'These days he could be hit by a car or run over by a combine harvester.'

'And I'm not sure I even remember how to be a parent,' said Corve. 'We're far too ancient and set in our ways. Aren't we Lilly?'

'Hmnnn,' said Lilly and passed the baby to Victor.

'Perhaps we should call Peter,' I said. 'This sounds like something the Folly would handle.'

'I don't see why we should be running to London every time we have a little problem up here,' said Miss Tefeidiad with a sniff. 'We've been solving our own problems for thousands of years—even if things have become complicated of late.'

'Social services, then,' I said.

'Absolutely not,' said Miss Tefeidiad.

'But he needs to be adopted,' said Lilly. 'That's the modern way.'

'If you say so,' said her mother.

I looked over to where Victor had plonked the boy down on the table and was making farting noises to keep him amused.

'He'll have to go to school,' said Corve.

'I don't see why,' said Miss Tefeidiad, 'I can't be doing with all this education.'

'He'll be able to make friends,' said Lilly. 'And blend in and move in a mysterious way.'

'You don't need an education to move in a mysterious way,' muttered Miss Tefeidiad.

'What we need is a nice local couple,' said Corve.

Ah, I thought, here it comes.

'I taught myself how to move in a mysterious way,' Miss Tefeidiad continued muttering.

'Childless for preference,' said Lilly.

'I don't see why we have to be mysterious in any case.'

'Good, solid respectable people,' said Corve.

'We never had to be respectable in the old days.'

'Pillars of the community,' said Lilly and winked at me.

'People had to be respectable to us.'

'With the appropriate level of resources,' said Corve.

'Newly married perhaps,' said Lilly, and all three mothers and daughters turned as one to smile at us.

'No,' I said, but I knew it was probably too late.

'How much influence will he have?' asked Victor.

'Influence on what?' asked Lilly.

'The weather, soil structure, lamb survival rates,' said Victor and I wondered, not for the first time, whether all farmers become obsessed or if only obsessive people become farmers.

Corve hesitated.

'Oh, tons of influence,' said Lilly quickly. 'Where his feet pass crops will grow, et cetera, et cetera.'

'And we're not without influence ourselves,' said Miss Tefeidiad.

'Yeah,' said Corve, 'We'd help out.'

'We'd be like his fairy godmothers,' said Lilly.

Victor caught my eye and raised an eyebrow.

Hail Dominic and Victor, the foxes had hailed us, soon to be blessed above all other minor landowners in Herefordshire and the wider border regions. The little bastards could have given us more of a warning.

'He seems like a good little chap,' said Victor.

'Victor,' I said slowly. 'He's the god of the River Lugg.'

'Good. He can help with the drainage then,' said Victor.

'And with a pair of fine upstanding men like you for parents,' said Miss Tefeidiad, 'what could possibly go wrong?'

At which point the baby Lugg peed on the table.

The Moments

Introduction

Sometimes you have an idea for something that is more of a mood than a story, something that will last a page or two and conjure an atmosphere. I decided to call these 'moments' and I include them in this volume for completeness.

Moment One
Nightingale—London September 1966

Since the war it had become impossible, during his infrequent visits to London, to persuade Hugh to visit the Folly, so we naturally gravitated to the Navy and Military. The food was not a patch on Molly's but like most of the survivors Hugh complained that there were too many ghosts at Russell Square for him to be truly comfortable.

'I'm surprised that you stay there yourself,' he'd said on an earlier trip. 'But then you were always made of sterner stuff than us mere mortals.'

The chaps have always needed to set me on a plinth this way. I can see it in their eyes. If the Nightingale can take it so can I, they say and who am I to disabuse them or tell them of the nights I have spent pleading with the spirits for some peace. If only there were ghosts in truth, after all I had been educated in a dozen different ways to rid myself of those.

I, of course, could not abandon the Folly without first abandoning Molly and that was not something I was prepared to do. This duty had proved a strong enough thread upon which to hang my sanity, that and the stubborn streak I had no doubt inherited from my mother.

Hugh was in fine fettle, that afternoon his son had recently taken a position with an old established firm in Hereford.

'One had feared that he would be drawn to the bright lights of the Metropolis,' said Hugh. 'Instead I am graced by his presence most weekends. He's taken a great interest in the bees of late.'

'And how are the hives,' I asked.

'Thriving naturally,' said Hugh. 'I have a talent if I do say so myself.'

I've always thought Hugh's desperate striving for normality was undermined by that strange quixotic urge of his. I've seen photographs of his 'tower' in Herefordshire and his interest in insects predated the war. David used to rag him mercilessly about his frequent field trips abroad.

'Hugh is our modern Darwin,' he once said. 'Only he takes his inspiration from beetles not snails.'

I remember Hugh in those dark forests on the Ettersberg. He'd dropped his staff and picked up a rifle. With every action of the bolt he swore at the German infantry as if they were responsible for the things we'd seen.

We all reached the limitations of our art that night.

'And speaking of our mighty capital,' said Hugh over our Castle Puddings. 'I've been hearing the most extraordinary things. The gypsies who came for the harvest this year said that there was a woman who has been claiming to be goddess of the River Thames. A coloured lady no less.' Hugh grinned and waves his fork as if it was my fault. 'Is this true? Is it even possible?'

I said that it seemed entirely possible and that I had met the young lady in question and she seemed entirely agreeable, if somewhat forceful. Hugh expressed interest in how the Old Man of the River might be taking this new turn of events and I told him with the same indifference he'd shown to events below Teddington Lock these last hundred years or so.

'I thought the old town felt different,' said Hugh and I felt a sudden moment of unwarranted alarm.

'Different in what way?' I asked.

'Oh, I don't know,' said Hugh. 'A certain frisson, a sense of excitement, youth, energy,' he trailed off and shrugged.

'The miniskirts?' I said because Hugh had always had an eye for the ladies.

'You don't feel it then?'

'I can't say that I do.'

'And yet you seem much more cheerful,' said Hugh. 'Has something changed?'

'You remember what David used to say—"everything is change".'

'I remember that you invariably responded with *plus ça change, plus c'est la même chose*,' said Hugh. 'Perhaps you were both right.'

After lunch I gave Hugh a lift to Paddington to catch his train. During the drive he suggested that I might trade in my perfectly serviceable Rover P4 for something more modern and went as far as to quote Marcus Aurelius—in the original Greek no less.

Dwell on the beauty of life. Watch the stars and see yourself running with them.

I hardly saw what that had to do with my choice of automobile but once he'd the idea in my head I began to see the advantages of perhaps acquiring one of the new model Jaguars. At the very least it would impress my colleagues at Scotland Yard.

And perhaps a new suit in the modern style to go with it.

Moment Two
Reynolds—Florence, Az. 2014

There's something about these motels that makes me want to talk to Jesus.

When I was a girl, I used to talk to him all the time, before races, exams, the occasional date—we used to be much closer. I had a friend in Jesus indeed. I suppose I stopped being so chatty as I got older. I reckoned Jesus did not need to know about every traffic jam on the way into the office, every burst pipe, lost cat, disappointing boyfriend—every trivial bump in my life. It's not that I stopped thinking that Jesus loved me, I know that he loves me as he loves all of us, I just felt he might have more important concerns. The world being what it is.

Still there's something about these motel rooms that make me want to get down on my knees and pray, head down, eyes closed or as my Mama used to say—adopting the right attitude towards the Lord.

I'm tempted to call Mama and talk to her instead, but she wouldn't understand and in any event, I'm not supposed to discuss these cases with civilians. Not even my Mama. She'd probably tell me to stop overthinking things and count my blessings. Which I do on a regular basis.

The motel room is painted a pale blue, there's a microwave on top of the minibar and an old-fashioned TV that promises cable at a price. The bedspread has an old-fashioned floral pattern in grey and green. The bed is nice and firm, which I like because when the Bureau send you out they don't spring for anything but coach. Although you'd be surprised how often the badge gets me an upgrade, especially out west. The air conditioning is good, thank God, and the Wi-Fi is decent.

Only the bed and the microwave are any temptation.

Florence has a main street called Main Street, a high school football team called the Gophers, a saloon that dates back to the Old West and seven different prisons. Incarceration is the local industry here and business is booming as criminals keep breaking the law and we keep locking them up. I've seen a great number of prisons on this assignment and the towns they sit next to are just ordinary small towns with ordinary folks doing ordinary things.

According to Google there are some restaurants on

Main Street but that would mean eating alone and that usually means having to fend off conversation. I was a much friendlier person at the start of this trip.

I keep imagining what it might be like to be sitting in a booth somewhere, my Kindle propped up against the napkin holder, wondering whether to have the peach cobbler or the apple pie. Then hearing that pop pop pop sound in the distance, or a scream, or seeing the waitress fall down and realise that you haven't even heard the gunshot. Hauling out my pistol, looking for a target, trying not to get shot.

I've only ever discharged my firearm in anger the one time and that was in a sewer under London, England and I missed the target.

When I was training at Quantico, I always imagined the silhouettes as bank robbers or terrorists or kidnappers but the men and women I visit in the prisons are so ordinary. Disgruntled high schoolers, angry ex-employees, ex-husbands. These are the ones that survive, mind you. The ones that surrender to their teacher or the first LEO on the scene or get overpowered by some brave folks using pepper spray or other improvised weapons. The other half of them get themselves shot or eat their own gun. No telling what they were like in person but from their files they seem as ordinary as anybody else.

There's all sorts of theories about why people become active shooters, but truth is nobody really knows the why. Only that they're getting more frequent and more deadly. My Mama says that it is a sign of the end times, but she said that the day Obama got elected for his second term and also that time during the superbowl when Janet Jackson had her wardrobe malfunction.

So now I've been sent out to see if there's anything supernatural about these killings. I do not believe they are going to be happy with my report because as far as I can tell a more natural bunch of murderers you will never find.

My Mama always said that if something magical weren't a miracle from God then it must be the work of the Devil but if he's behind these shootings he's too subtle for me.

So first thing tomorrow I'm going to visit one of those seven prisons and interview a thirty six year old white male who shot his wife and his mother in law and was all set to shoot up his home town if he hadn't been tackled by, of all people, the mail man. He barely made the local news.

The motel room is blue and I think I'm going to have quick talk with Jesus.

It's that or the emergency box of Pizza Rolls I have in my case.

Moment Three
Tobias Winter—Meckenheim 2012

I'd only been back at Meckenheim for a couple of days when the reports arrived from London. I'd been out in the East, in Radeburg, recovering a Case White artefact that the local police had uncovered from a suspected Werewolf cache. Don't let the name excite you, these jobs are always the same. I drive across the country, sign for a sealed package and drive back. I rarely get to spend even a night out on the town because the local boys can't hustle me out of their jurisdiction fast enough. You'd think the bloody things were radioactive, they're not you know, early on I 'borrowed' a Geiger counter from the forensics lot and started checking them before I put them in the car.

Judging from the weight and size of the package I'm relatively certain that it was a diary or ledger. If so, I was in no doubt that my next task would be to scour through it for names to add to our database. My chief has often complained that our obsession with the Nazi past is holding us back. It's certainly generated enough paperwork.

'Sooner or later this national obsession has to pass,' she said once. 'We've all become far too comfortable playing this role.'

Although she's never once said what exactly it was holding us back from and I for one was not in a hurry to find out. Like my father I favour a comfortable Germany, it's about the only thing we've ever agreed on.

I didn't ask to join the Department for Complex and Unspecific Matters, in fact I made a spirited attempt to blow the interview. When the Chief asked me why I'd joined the Bundeskriminalamt I told her it was because they wouldn't have me in Cobra 11. That should have been it but instead the Chief smiled her terrifying smile.

'You'll do nicely,' she said.

When we're not transporting dangerous artefacts or chasing rumours of possessed BMWs, never Mercedes for some reason, we work office hours at the KDA. I like to get in at eight. So I get an hour to myself before the Chief and the administration team arrive so I wasn't best pleased to find an email from the secure communications section informing that they had a message for me. Protocol dictates that I collect such documents myself, so down I went to the basement. I read the first page summary while I was still in the secure communications room. Then I asked the officer in charge to send a message back to London.

'Can't you send an email?' he asked.

'Not for this,' I said.

They don't have chairs in the waiting area of the communications section, so I propped up the wall and speed read the bulk of the message while I was waiting for a reply. When it came I put both in my secure briefcase and took them upstairs.

The Abteilung KDA was once a much bigger section and as a result we have a large number of empty offices at our end of the second floor. The fact that none of the departments have tried to appropriate them for their own officers should tell you something about how we are regarded by the rest of the Bundeskriminalamt.

I found the Chief in her office standing in front of the window looking out on her unrivalled view of the car park.

'The Nightingale has taken an apprentice,' I said.

The Chief is a tall, slender woman with a long pale face and red lips. She favours black skirt suits cut in a very elegant, old-fashioned style and I've heard her described as looking like the CEO of a corporation run by vampires.

I've faced a vampire and the only reason I'm able to talk about it now is because I was carrying a flame thrower at the time. So no, I think she looks like a woman who needs to get out in the sun more.

'Ah,' said the Chief. 'That's unfortunate. How certain is this?'

'The Embassy has confirmed it.'

She turned to check that I'd closed the door behind me and that nobody else could see or hear.

'Shit, shit, shit,' she said. 'Why is it always bloody London? I told them we needed someone at the Embassy full time.' She tapped a long blood red fingernail on her desk for a moment and then glanced back out of the window to see if the rain had stopped.

'Get my things,' she said. 'We're going for a walk.'

The Chief has a favourite smoking place amongst the trees at the far end of the athletics track. She smokes dreadful f6 cigarettes but I'm certain these are an affectation like her Saxon accent - part of her disguise.

'Details,' she said as she jammed a cigarette into her long black holder.

I summarised the summary. She interrupted me only once and that was so I could light her cigarette.

'What do we know about this Peter Grant?' she asked.

'African mother, English father, joined the London police two and a half years ago,' I said. 'The London Embassy have promised more in the next few days.'

The Chief stubbed her cigarette out on the nearest tree and jammed a fresh one into the holder.

'We should have had someone in London full time,' she said.

It had always been the consensus in the Federal Government that the supernatural had been 'contained' and the KDA's job was that of a glorified cleaning service. The Foreign Ministry wasn't about to allocate a valuable diplomatic position to someone whose job description could at best be described as 'hanging about in case something magical happens'.

Only now it had.

'Do they have more information on the murder?' she asked.

'Four murders now,' I said. 'One of the victims was an infant. They're sure the case is linked to Nightingale breaking the agreement, but they don't know why.'

'So much for "contained",' said the Chief. 'Do you know what this means?'

I've learnt not to interrupt the Chief when she's in full rhetorical flow.

'This means,' she said blowing smoke, 'that we'll have to expand our own capabilities to match.'

She looked at me in a way that did not entirely make me feel comfortable.

'Tobias,' she said.

'Ma'am?'

'Have you ever considered learning magic?'

Just one more thing...

Even as this volume is being beaten into shape by a copy-editor more short stories are being written and planned. There are many characters in the green room clamouring for their moment in the sun. Professor Postmartin and Hatbox Winstanley from 'A Rare Book Of Cunning Device' will be teaming up to track down witch's curses in Enfield and hunting unicorns in Havering. Winter and Sommer face a curious cold case in Schwerte while a shopkeeper in Redbridge has to negotiate a tricky deal with some talkative urban foxes.

So if you enjoyed these stories I can promise you more are on their way.

Until then, good luck, stay safe and keep the faith.

—Ben Aaronovitch, June 2020

About the Author

Born and raised in London, Ben Aaronovitch worked as a scriptwriter for *Doctor Who* and *Casualty* before the inspiration for his own series of books struck him whilst working as a bookseller in Waterstones Covent Garden. Ben Aaronovitch's unique novels are the culmination of his experience of writing about the emergency services and the supernatural.

Want to be the first to hear the news about the **Rivers of London** books?

Sign up to Ben Aaronovitch's newsletter at **https://bit.ly/BenNewsletter**

FOR NEWS ABOUT
JABBERWOCKY
BOOKS AND AUTHORS

Sign up for our newsletter*: http://eepurl.com/b84tDz
visit our website: awfulagent.com/ebooks
or follow us on twitter: @awfulagent

THANKS FOR READING!

*We will never sell or give away your email address, nor use
it for nefarious purposes. Newsletter sent out quarterly.

Printed in Great Britain
by Amazon

72798157R00142